*Hurricanes
over London*

Hurricanes over London

Charles Reid

RONSDALE PRESS

HURRICANES OVER LONDON
Copyright © 2001 Charles Reid
Reprinted April 2004

RONSDALE PRESS
3350 West 21st Avenue
Vancouver, B.C., Canada
V6S 1G7

Set in Minion: 12 pt on 16
Typesetting: Julie Cochrane
Printing: Hignell Printing, Winnipeg, Manitoba
Cover Art: Ljuba Levstek
Cover Design: Julie Cochrane

Ronsdale Press wishes to thank the Canada Council for the Arts, the Government of Canada through the Book Publishing Industry Development Program (BPIDP), and the Province of British Columbia through the British Columbia Arts Council for their support of its publishing program.

CANADIAN CATALOGUING IN PUBLICATION DATA
Reid, Charles, 1925–
    Hurricanes over London

    ISBN 0-921870-82-5

    1. World War, 1939–1945 — Aerial operations, British — Juvenile fiction. I. Title.
PS8585.E4485H87 2001   jC813'.6   C00-911196-4
PZ7.R265Hu 2001

*This book is dedicated
to all young Canadians, in the hope
that it will inspire them to search out more
of their country's history, and by so
doing realize that they need not look beyond
these shores for their heroes, for Canada
has an abundance of its own.*

ACKNOWLEDGEMENTS

My thanks to John Wilson, who put me on the right track for this book, to the Nanaimo Military Museum for the use of its excellent library, and to the Aerospace Museum for inspiring the creation of Jamie Davis' adventure.

1

The Notebook

Jamie Davis tugged at the unfamiliar collar for the umpteenth time, scuffling his shoes in the dirt around the grave. His mother glared and he stopped scuffling.

The vicar's voice droned on endlessly and Jamie wondered how much longer the man could go on and how he knew so much about Jamie's grandfather. Jamie himself knew very little and had shown even less interest on the times he had been taken to see his grandparents. It wasn't that they weren't nice. In fact they had always been very good to him. It was just that they always talked about the past and Jamie found it hard to relate to a London he had never seen and those funny little houses they talked about . . . and they all seemed to have been *so* poor.

Then there was the war. Always the war came up, a war that was so long ago even his father knew little about it *and* they certainly never mentioned it much in school. So Jamie had a tendency to let the talk flow over his head and think about Skippy and Tozer and his other friends, planning the things they were going to do once he could get home and get out of the "decent" clothes his mother always insisted he wore when they visited his grandparents.

"Come on Jamie." His mother's voice and the tug on his sleeve brought Jamie back to the present and he realized the service was over.

He looked into the grave where his grandfather's coffin rested. Soon he knew the dirt would be shovelled in and his grandfather would be gone. The thought disturbed him in some way he couldn't quite figure out and he quickly turned away, following his mother back to the sombre cars waiting at the cemetery gate.

The people babbled on incessantly, pausing only long enough to take another gulp of his grandfather's whisky or gobble one more of the tiny sandwiches his mother had risen at dawn to prepare.

Jamie stood ignored in the corner and wondered why it was necessary to feed all these people just because his grandfather had died and *why* they were *so* cheerful. Shouldn't they be sad or something?

He thought perhaps he ought to be sad, too, but found it

hard to keep his thoughts from the softball game he should have been playing that afternoon. "Bet they lose without my pitching," he muttered to himself, "and if Skippy strikes out again, I'll kill him." The gang often said this about Skippy but saying it today, in this room suddenly made Jamie feel uncomfortable.

"Well, I didn't *really* mean I'd kill him," he said quietly to himself and then he immediately felt better.

The noise seemed overwhelming in his grandmother's living room and Jamie wandered out into the hall where it was quieter. The door to his grandfather's study stood open. It wasn't really a study but a small bedroom that did double duty as a guest room.

Jamie pushed the door open and slowly went inside. He had never been in there before — not that it was out of bounds to him. It was just that he had never been interested in what his grandfather did in there.

Two walls were covered with books and a handmade desk filled one corner. On the desk was a computer. This took him by surprise, for the idea that his grandfather would know how to use a computer had never occurred to him.

The other wall contained the sofa that pulled out into a bed when the room was needed as a bedroom.

Walking over to the bookshelves Jamie looked more closely at the books. There was a full set written by Winston Churchill, one simply titled *Montgomery*, another called

General George S. Patton. On the spine of the next book were the words *Six Armies in Normandy.* Next to this was the story of Pearl Harbour. There were many others but these were the only ones even slightly familiar to Jamie.

Suddenly he noticed a plain black notebook at the end of one shelf and pulled it down.

He flicked idly through the pages. A sentence leapt out of one page, freezing Jamie's hand on the paper.

A shard of glass like a dagger was embedded in the woman's throat and her blood had trickled down over the baby's head.

Jamie flipped back to the front of the notebook. The first page had the words "This was my War" with his grandfather's name below the title.

He started reading the first page which was titled Prologue.

———

THE DAY MY COUNTRY WENT TO WAR

I tried to lean nonchalantly on our front gate alongside my father but when you are only three-feet-ten and the gate itself is three feet high, a nonchalant lean is hard to achieve, so I contented myself with stuffing my hands in my pockets and trying to look intelligent instead.

I remember Billy Batt's dad was there and Mr. Willcox

from next door. Then after a few minutes my uncle Jim and Sammy Napthali's dad hurried up the street and crowded round our gate. "WAR." The word crackled like a charge of electricity in the tranquil atmosphere of that September morning.

Of course, I knew all about war. I had seen John Wayne dozens of times striding like a colossus across the silver screen — oh yes, I knew all about war.

The weather that day gave no hint of the impending doom. No heavy clouds rolled across the sky, neither did lightning flash or thunder roar. Instead, the sun shone from a sky of perfect azure and the air had that heady scent that only autumn can bring. Not even a breeze disturbed the serenity of that Sunday — that day my country went to war.

—⁓—

Jamie read the page again and felt a tingling of anticipation. The story itself now seemed to begin.

—⁓—

We stood and stared at the huge hole that was appearing in our football pitch. Well, actually, it wasn't really a football pitch. It was just a large gravel-covered square surrounded by our houses but to us it was much, much more.

In the spring, it was where we flew our kites. In the summer, it was where we played cricket. But perhaps most important of all it was where, on Guy Fawkes night, our bonfire stood, rising to rooftop height and towering above those of all other gangs in our part of London's East End. It was said that when fully alight, the flames could be seen from London Bridge several miles to the west.

To create this monster, we would spend most of the summer holidays hunting down wood and anything else burnable from all over the area. Once we went to an engineering firm several miles away and they gave us a huge packing case that had housed a new piece of machinery. We literally dragged this giant piece of fuel all the way home, such was the importance of that bonfire to us.

Our street had two types of houses. On one side of the square were the new red brick council houses that we had all moved into around three years ago. The other side of the square consisted of the original older houses with their low brick walls topped by wrought iron railings and enclosed with wrought iron gates, all soon to disappear as fodder for the factories making guns and tanks.

The day we moved into our new home was quite a "red letter" day, for that day my father got his first real job since the Depression seven years before. It would also be the first time we had ever lived in a real house, all our previous years having been spent in an ancient block of flats built over the canal in Stratford High Street.

I remember we had to move our meagre belongings on a handcart, the type used by stallholders at the market. I also remember standing open-mouthed at one particular room in the new house, for I had never seen a bathroom before. All we had in the block of flats was one toilet for each floor and bath nights were a once-a-week event in a tin tub.

This, with my father now in regular work for the first time since the Depression, was the beginning of three magical years for us all, with wonderful family Christmases and brand new toys instead of second-hand cast-offs for us children.

—*m*—

"Jamie."

Jamie came to with a start and whirled around. His grandmother was standing in the doorway smiling at him, although to Jamie her smile seemed forlorn.

"Gran, what's Guy Fawkes?"

"What brought that up?" replied Jamie's grandmother, somewhat surprised.

"It was in this — something Grandpa wrote." Jamie held up the notebook.

Jamie's grandmother's smile suddenly became less forlorn. "Oh, I see you've found your grandfather's story about his misspent youth. He always said he would publish it one day." She paused for a moment, reflectively, then continued.

"Guy Fawkes is a very big day for children in Britain, like Halloween is here."

"But what is it for? Grandpa talks about this huge bonfire."

"Well, hundreds of years ago, this man named Fawkes tried to blow up the Parliament building by planting gunpowder in the basement but he was caught and hanged for treason. Ever since then, on November the fifth, the day it happened, people have had bonfires on which they burn an effigy of Guy Fawkes and let off loads of fireworks. I expect your grandfather was talking about the one in their street, was he? I believe it was the biggest in East London and he once told me that sometimes they sent a fire tender to watch over it."

"Gran, can I take this home and read it. It's kinda interesting."

Jamie's grandmother looked pleased. "If you are interested, you can keep it as a memento of your grandfather."

"Thanks Gran."

Jamie left the room with his grandmother, stuffing the notebook into his raincoat pocket that was hanging in the hall.

Back in the living room, Jamie was surprised to find it almost empty. His mother was clearing away the last of the dishes and his father was saying goodbye to the last person there.

Jamie gave a quick look at the clock. If we leave soon, he thought, I can still get to the diamond before they leave.

"Shall I get my coat, mum?"

"In a few minutes."

Jamie watched the clock anxiously as precious minutes

seemed to fly by. He wondered how the minutes that went so slowly at the cemetery were now going so fast.

Finally, his mother and father were ready and with some last farewells and a promise extracted from his grandmother that she was to join them for supper, Jamie and his parents left for home.

"We lost," Freddie said before Jamie could ask. "Yeah and Skippy struck out again," Tozer put in, disgust in his voice.

Freddie was small, wiry and intelligent, the exact opposite of Tozer, who dwarfed them all.

"I tried Jamie, honest." Skippy looked near to tears.

"Aw, forget it." Jamie still felt guilty about his thoughts at his grandfather's funeral so, although seething inside, he smiled at Skippy, clapped him on the shoulder, and said, "Let's go get a Coke."

2

The Gathering Storm

The rain that had threatened all through the funeral finally arrived the next morning.

"No ball practice today," Jamie said to himself as he pulled on his jacket. It was then he glimpsed the notebook sticking out of his raincoat pocket. On the spur of the moment he took it out and stuffed it into the pocket of his jacket.

"Bye mum," he called out as he slammed the door and bent his head into the driving rain.

The rain showed no sign of letting up when lunch time came around, so Jamie found himself a quiet corner and, with his sandwiches in front of him, pulled the notebook from his pocket. He re-read the bit about Guy Fawkes and the bonfire and wondered what the hole being dug was all about. He found out in the first sentence as the story continued.

———

"Building a shelter," my cousin Jimmy said unnecessarily.

"Looks like we'll have to use the tip," I put in, referring to the waste ground on the north side of our housing development.

"Can't." This was Puddy Skittrel, the largest member of our gang. Puddy's real name was Cecil but no one with any sense ever called him that.

———

Sounds like Tozer, Jamie thought, smiling.

———

"Why not?"

"Going to turn it into allotments . . . get everyone growing vegetables and things . . . heard my dad talking." Puddy liked to use this cryptic way of talking. He thought it made him sound like Jimmy Cagney.

We all stood and watched the hole growing larger by the minute, stunned into silence by this major catastrophe.

As each day went by, we had to watch as our "exclusive" playground disappeared and was replaced by a vast tunnel-like building, most of which was buried in the large hole dug out by the workmen. Long sloping ramps went down to its two entrances, each closed in with a large steel door.

—⁓—

Jamie's interest suddenly increased as he turned the page and a new chapter began.

—⁓—

"Blimey, I'd love to get Sally Hoggs down 'ere." We were sitting in the now completed air-raid shelter, with its rows of wooden bunks and ghostly lighting. The steel doors had been left open to allow for a quick entry should a raid occur, so we were able to just walk in and inspect this monster. At that moment we were sprawled out on a couple of the wooden bunks that lined the walls from one entrance to the other. It was Sammy Napthali who had put all our thoughts into words — Sammy with the dark curly hair that no brush or comb could tame, Sammy of the dumb questions and the big heart.

Sally Hoggs was the local flirt. At fifteen she was just blossoming into womanhood and had every boy in the street chasing her, but in our age group she was considered an unattainable dream. Still, everyone grinned and put on that knowing look of fourteen-year-olds, back in the more innocent days of 1939 — that knowing look that said we knew it all — when in reality, we knew nothing.

—⁓—

Jamie paused and looked up. "Gosh," he marvelled aloud, "Grandpa was only as old as me when the war started." He continued eagerly.

———

"Some bleedin' hope you got, Sammy," Puddy said, grinning.

"I wouldn't mind trying though," Danny said, echoing all our thoughts. Danny, like us all, had been born right here, in London's East End but his voice had the soft Irish lilt of his mother's birthplace. He also had more than his share of smarts.

"Why don't we have a bet on it," my cousin Jimmy piped in.

"Geez, if I get Sally Hoggs down 'ere, you can keep any bleedin' money," Sammy broke back in and everyone burst out laughing.

"How much shall we make it then — tanner each?"

We all now stopped and looked at Puddy. None of us had been thinking that big. After all, sixpence was a lot of money. It was a day at the pictures with pie and mash after.

"Whatsa matter? Ain't you so confident any more . . . tell you what, I'll cover the bet. That means the winner gets three bob, including his bet." Puddy looked straight at Sammy.

———

Jamie made a mental note to ask his grandmother what these tanners and bobs were, then continued eagerly.

—⁓—

"I'm in," Danny's soft brogue broke the silence.

"Me too," I burst out before Puddy got around to me.

"Course I'm in," Sammy found his voice at last.

Puddy's eyes swivelled round to my cousin Jimmy.

"Well," he almost snarled.

My cousin produced a sickly smile. He was not Puddy's favourite gang member.

"Course I'm in, was my idea wasn't it."

"Right, let's say by Sunday then."

Everyone nodded and we trooped out of the shelter.

—⁓—

"*Jamie,*" Jamie was so engrossed that it wasn't until Freddie punched him playfully on the shoulder that he realized Freddie, Tozer and Skippy were all staring down at him, "where you been? We've been looking all over for you."

"Nowhere. Just sitting here reading."

"Whatcha reading?"

"Oh nothing." Jamie, knowing Tozer's certain reaction, stuffed the book back into his pocket. Just then the bell went for afternoon class and he was spared any more explanation.

On the way home from school, Jamie decided to call in on his grandmother. He knew she would give him a hot drink and then he could ask about the "tanners and bobs" his grandfather had talked about.

"Jamie, what a nice surprise. You must be soaked. Come in and I'll make you some hot chocolate."

Jamie peeled off his wet jacket.

"Thanks, Gran." Jamie sipped at the steaming chocolate before asking his question. "Gran, what is a tanner, a bob and a sixpence?"

Jamie's grandmother looked pleased. "So, you *are* reading that notebook of your grandfather?"

"Yeah, it's quite interesting but some of the words he uses don't mean anything."

"Oh, I expect you'll come across a lot of those. Well, tanner is just a slang word for sixpence, so they mean the same. It was worth six pennies, and a bob, or shilling as it really was, was worth twelve pennies."

"So one's worth a bit more than a nickel and the shilling just over a dime. That's not much is it?" Jamie was thinking they *must* have been poor to make such a fuss about so small a bet.

"Well no, it was worth a bit more than that because an English penny is worth more than our penny, Jamie, and it was still a lot of money to a boy back then."

Jamie finished his drink. "Thanks, Gran. I'd better be getting home now."

"You're welcome, Jamie. I like to see you, and I'm glad you're enjoying the story. Just call round when you find something else you don't understand."

"I will, Gran, and thanks again." Jamie zipped up his jacket and went out into the rain, which was still falling heavily.

That night after supper Jamie's mother and father settled down, as they normally did, to watch television and Jamie did what he normally did if he wasn't going out — scooted up to his room. Except that tonight once he had closed the door and settled down he ignored his C.D. player and opened up his grandfather's notebook and turned eagerly to the page he had marked.

—◁◁◁—

"Well, tell us then, what happened?" It was Sammy, his eyes popping with anticipation, who shouted the question as everyone crowded round Danny and me.

It was Sunday night and we were back in the shelter that had already become our headquarters. In those early days of the war — a war that seemed such a joke — we had exclusive use of it.

Danny and I had actually succeeded in persuading Sally Hoggs down into the shelter the night before — well actually it was Danny's Irish charm that did it. I just happened to be there.

Danny and I smirked at each other, keeping the suspense going a little longer.

"Well, are you going to tell us or not?" Puddy snarled.

I could not contain myself any longer. "Boy, does she know how to kiss," I burst out with all the *savoir faire* of the man of the world.

"Yeah," Danny broke in, "I couldn't believe it."

"Whadya mean?" Puddy snapped back.

"Well it was all sort of wet and soft," I put in.

"Sounds a bit sloppy to me," Sammy said, a disappointed look on his face.

"You wouldn't say that if it was *you* being kissed," Danny answered.

"Yeah, I'm telling you it was something else," I put in.

"And?" Puddy was looking at us both with a slightly bored expression, obviously waiting for the meaty part of the story.

"Well, I got my hand on her knee," Danny said with as much excitement as he could.

I don't know whether this was true or not because after the kiss, Sally had curled her warm fingers through mine and I was oblivious to everything else, but I do remember the pistol-like crack as Sally's hand smacked Danny's cheek. I also remember being very annoyed at the time with Danny, for ruining my first romantic interlude but I kept my mouth shut, leaving him to decide if he wanted to reveal his embarrassment.

"*And*?" my cousin Jimmy spoke for the first time.

"She got up and ran out." Danny's voice was full of disgust.

"Blimey, is that it?" Puddy said. "I thought we were going to hear something real juicy."

"Yeah, well Puddy, it's more than you ever got, right Charlie?"

"Too right, Danny, and I reckon if she hadn't run out we'd have got more," I replied vehemently, although I had little idea of what "more" might have consisted of.

We held our hands out for the money. Even though we had had our moment of glory, a shilling each was a lot of money plus of course our original bets back.

Puddy could not totally hide his fury as he doled out the money, obviously only making the offer to cover the bet in the first place because he was convinced none of us could win and he would pocket an easy two shillings from our lost bets.

———

Jamie paused and stared at the ceiling as he tried to imagine the quiet, homely old man he knew chasing girls but found he could not quite capture the picture. He shook his head and returned to the story and found his grandfather had moved on again.

———

The eye piece fogged up and the stink of rubber made me want to puke but I didn't care. I had my very own gas mask. Now, I was really part of this war.

The rest of the gang had been swanking around with theirs for weeks but Puddy and I, being R and S in the alphabet, were at the tail-end of the list. My mother had already purchased the little plastic cases that had appeared miraculously in every store and I proudly stowed my mask away and slung it over my shoulder as if it were a gun. The Air Raid Warden was giving us final instructions and warning us to carry them everywhere. Was he kidding? For the next year, until it became *passé* and the *real* way to show you were a man was to leave it at home, I practically slept with it. This was the closest any of us were to come to war for almost a year as the mighty German war machine inexplicably slumbered through that first winter, leaving us to brag about what we were going to do to Hitler and revel in such silly songs as "We're gonna hang out the washing on the Siegfried Line," Germany's defence line facing the fabled, but soon to be made obsolete, French Maginot Line.

Jamie paused again and tried to grasp what it was like to live with the fear of being gassed. He knew enough about this kind of warfare to know people could die horribly from the gas and he marvelled at the casual approach obviously taken by his grandfather and his friends. He wondered if the grown-ups had had the same attitude and how his father and mother might react to such a situation. Don't think they'd be very calm, he thought to himself with a smile.

His grandfather had moved on yet again to another part of the story and this one grabbed Jamie's attention immediately.

———

"Quick Charlie, come and see. They tried to launch a barrage balloon from the square and it nosedived into the cut. The cable's broke all our side gate and smashed my dad's dahlias. You should hear him bollocking the sergeant."

Cousin Jimmy's face was flushed with excitement and he took off at a run. I slung my gas mask to the back and pelted after him.

A young and very white-faced Air Force sergeant and my Uncle Jim were surrounded by half the street.

Several privates were standing around, looking helplessly at the huge cable lying across Uncle Jim's wrecked side gate and snaking through the remains of his prize dahlias before disappearing over the back fence.

Uncle Jim's face was bright red and his fist was jammed against the young sergeant's nose.

"You stupid idiot, look what you've done to my dahlias. Whose going to pay for this bleedin' mess, eh?"

"I'm sorry, sir. We never expected it to do that. I'm sure you'll be compensated."

But Uncle Jim was not to be mollified. "Lot of bleedin' good that'll do. What the cable didn't break, those flat-footed idiots ran all over — and get that . . ." The expletive died on Uncle Jim's lips as he caught sight of Aunt Kate's tightly folded arms and thinly pursed lips, leaving him spluttering lamely, "that — cable out of my garden." Then storming past Aunt Kate, he strode into the house.

"Geez, is your dad ever mad," Sammy's voice was full of awe. "Glad it wasn't me smashed his dahlias."

"Yeah, ain't he. Bet my mum's giving him hell for losing his temper like that though. Come on, let's go round to the cut and see the balloon."

We all raced around to the footpath that ran behind the houses and alongside the canal.

The sergeant was left trying to marshall his grinning crew. "Right men, line up now." His voice rose to a falsetto as he tried to regain some lost authority, "QUICK MARCH."

The half-inflated barrage balloon was draped across the footpath and hanging from the fence on the other side, with the larger portion floating in the water.

"PLATOON-HALT." The sergeant brought his crew to a standstill. "Now men, let's get this 'ere balloon out of the water. Look smart now."

First of all they tried grabbing the trailing ropes and pulling on the balloon, but all it did was flop up and down like some huge overgrown jellyfish.

"Ain't never gonna move it like that!" Sammy yelled as

Jimmy and I nearly fell over the railings with laughter at the antics of the airmen.

"Now you mind your own business, sonny." The sergeant glared at Sammy, then turned back to his men. "*Come on now*, put some beef into it."

Muttering curses, the sweating men heaved harder on the ropes and this time the balloon surged higher out of the water.

"That's it men, keep pulling, it's coming."

Suddenly the balloon flopped back into the canal, dragging the men forward. The two at the front, unable to let go in time, shot forward as if fired from a gun, flew over the railings, and went head first into the canal.

"Oh Geez, will you look at that," Sammy gasped as the tears rolled down our cheeks.

Sammy regained his breath. "Eh Sarge, thought you guys were Air Force, not Navy."

The sergeant, who was peering down into the canal, looked up and glared, then turning, spoke to one of his men. "Get over the side and give those two a hand."

"What me, Sarge, I can't bleedin' swim."

"Alright, *you Smith*."

The private called Smith reluctantly climbed over the railing and started to slide down the canal bank to where the other two were floundering around in the shallow water, yelling for help.

"There goes number three!" we all yelled as airman

Smith's feet began to slip on the muddy bank and he gathered speed, shooting faster and faster down the bank, hitting the water feet first and sliding up to his waist in the slimy sludge.

"Right on Sarge," we all chorused through our tears of laughter, "way to go."

The sergeant glared silently at us again.

"Right, Sidney, get over there and help."

The man Sidney didn't even fare as well as the previous one, losing his footing almost immediately and shooting into the canal face first. He clawed his way upright, mud plastered all over his face.

"Sergeant!" — a baby-faced lieutenant was striding down the canal path.

"What the hell is going — oh my God." The lieutenant stopped, staring at the barrage balloon and the mud-covered men silently for about a minute, then his eyes followed the cable snaking away over Uncle Jim's back fence.

Bringing his eyes back to the sergeant, he said quietly, "Cut the damn thing loose. We'll send a working party out tomorrow to fish it out. And get that bloody cable out of that man's garden before he sees it and gives somebody hell."

With that, he turned and strode away, leaving the hapless sergeant saluting his departing back.

Needless to say, we never saw the balloon again but that remaining part of our old football pitch must have had a fascination for someone because two days later an anti-air-craft gun was hauled on to it. After several hours manoeu-vring the gun into place, the crew decided to have a prac-tice shoot. The first salvo blew out half the windows in the street and brought poor old Mrs. Cox (whose mind was more than a little vague) running out of her house, scream-ing "pison gas–pison gas," at the top of her lungs.

After this latest debacle, they finally gave up on the idea of using that piece of ground and left us in peace.

—◆—

Jamie wiped away his own tears of laughter as he closed the book, "Boy, I would have loved to have seen that," he muttered, turning out the light.

"You're *not* going to practise today?" Tozer's voice was incredulous as he tried to grasp the fact that someone could find anything better to do than play ball.

"No, like I said, I got something I gotta do." With that Jamie scuttled off, leaving his friends staring at his depart-ing back.

"Gran, what was it *really* like, being in the war?" Jamie asked after taking a sip of the hot chocolate his grand-mother had just brought him.

His grandmother smiled. "Well, I wasn't in London like your grandfather, so I did not see what he saw. Also, I was much younger. I remember ration books and the fact that we hardly ever had sweets or butter, or things like that. And, of course, new clothes were just something we saw in magazines. Most of my school clothes were made out of old cut-up dresses of my mother's."

"They seemed to be so casual about it all. In one bit of the story, Grandpa talks about getting a gas mask and makes it all sound like good fun." Jamie looked enquiringly at his grandmother.

"Well, don't forget that in the early days, especially to young boys, it *was* one big adventure but I suspect the story won't be all like that. I remember some of the things he told me later were much more serious."

Jamie was to remember that remark as he got further into his grandfather's story.

———

"Don't suppose you'll be 'aving your Christmas party this year, Charlie?"

Our Christmas party had grown up over the last three years, by accident really. First, one family of relatives came and then it seemed the next year everyone turned up. Our small council house only had three bedrooms but during the Christmas to New Year period, around twelve extra bodies were accommodated.

The men would go to their jobs each day and come back to start another party, the whole thing lasting until New Year's day.

"Of course we'll have it," replied Charlie. "Everybody's bringing their ration cards round to my mum and she's going to do everything, and I bet my grandad gets a chicken from somewhere."

"But you *can't* put all your lights up, can you?" asked Sammy.

Puddy withered Sammy with a look. "Don't be bleedin' daft, of course they can't. You really think your grandad can get a chicken, Charlie?"

"Sure he can, Puddy. There ain't nobody 'e don't know down Petticoat Lane."

My grandfather was 92 pounds of wrinkled leather with that kind of walnut tan that is only seen on people who live their lives outdoors. People in the East End called him a cunning old horse trader, although I didn't understand what this meant for a long time.

He lived with my Aunt Kate and Uncle Jim, having given up his old house in Stratford High Street when my grandmother died.

There was a story my mother told about something that happened before he moved. In those early days when he was alone, Aunt Kate used to go round once a week and clean the house for him.

Now, my grandfather, like many of his generation, had an inherent mistrust of banks, so, according to my mother, he kept his savings in an old canvas bag which he used to hide in the chimney of a disused fireplace.

On one of her cleaning visits my Aunt Kate decided to clean the chimney of the old fireplace and the bag tumbled out. Aunt Kate apparently took the bag down to the end of the yard and tossed it into the canal that ran by the house. Whatever possessed her to do such a thing was never explained but I do recall my mother would always give an odd sort of smile when she reached this part of the story.

Anyway, just as Aunt Kate came back to the house, my grandfather arrived home. He took one look at the fireplace and screamed at her, "where's my bag?" At her reply, he ran down the yard and jumped straight into the canal and fished out his precious bag.

My mother said he spent the whole evening carefully ironing his money dry. Whether this story is true or not, I never knew but I do remember him charging round our street with his horse and cart, from which he would sell bags of peanuts to the kids. Once he bought a goat and tied it to the lampost outside my aunt and uncle's house much to my aunt's disgust, because she was a stickler for neatness and cleanliness. The real crunch came when the goat started trying to "goose" her every time she went in and out of the gate. Very soon after that the goat disappeared.

My cockiness over the chicken came from many Sundays spent at Petticoat Lane with my father and grandfather where, on arrival at the livestock stalls, my grandfather would push himself through the crowds and, once at the front of a particular stall, would keep up a constant barrage of criticism of the chickens being sold until the harassed trader would sell him a pair of his prize cockerels at a knockdown price, just to get rid of him.

"Is your Uncle Dick and Uncle Alf coming?" Sammy put in. "Geez I'll never forget when they dressed up as little girls last year and went round the pub to buy some beer."

My two uncles were favourites of us all, especially my Uncle Dick, who was every boy's idea of what he would like to be when he grew up — tall, darkly handsome, with jet black, laughing eyes and an insatiable appetite for fun.

"Course, and Uncle Dick will be bringing his drums and my brother and Johnny Tozeland will be there with their accordions, so we'll have the band like always."

"What about your Aunt Nell? She's something else on the piano."

I laughed at Danny. "Blimey, you couldn't keep her away from a party."

My Aunt Nell was a huge woman who seemed to be able to do anything she put her mind to. She could knit like lightning, read a book and carry on a conversation, all at the same time. Sometimes she would come round to our house on a Saturday night and ask one of us boys if we would like a new pullover and by the time she left we would be wearing it.

The war that Christmas continued to be a non-event, the only outward signs being the air-raid shelters, ration cards, the blackout and lots more uniforms. My dad and elder brother were both in the Red Cross and Uncle Dick, the Auxiliary Fire Service, but all in all, we barely noticed the difference in our Christmas party, which still managed to go on until New Year's day.

3

Young Soldiers

"Would you like some cookies? I have just made a fresh batch," Jamie's grandmother called from the kitchen.

"Yes please, Gran." The smell of fresh baking wafted in from the kitchen and Jamie surprised himself with the thought that he actually enjoyed these visits, even without his grandfather's story to talk about.

"These are great, Gran," he mumbled, his mouth full of the fresh delicious taste.

"Glad you like them," his grandmother replied, looking at Jamie with a questioning glance. "Have you found something else in the story to ask me about?"

"Well — yes Gran, but I wanted to come round anyway."

"I'm glad, dear." His grandmother smiled. "So what has your grandfather come up with this time?"

"Well, he talks about his family and the Christmas parties they had — Gee, that must have been fun, Gran."

"Oh yes, they seemed to be quite a family with lots of talent and full of fun. If he was talking about Christmas, he must have mentioned his grandfather and Petticoat Lane."

"Yes, he does. What a funny name, Gran."

Jamie's grandmother smiled, "Ah Petticoat Lane. Yes it is a funny name but it was not its real name. Petticoat Lane was actually a street called Brick Lane. It was in Whitechapel in the East End of London."

"So why did they call it Petticoat Lane?"

"Well, they had a huge street market there every Sunday and although it later sold everything, it started out as a second-hand clothes market that sold mainly women's clothes. I'll bet you've been reading about the chickens," Jamie's grandmother chuckled but there was a far-away look in her eyes. Suddenly she spoke again. "Does he mention the pickpockets?"

"No, Gran," said Jamie, immediately intrigued.

His grandmother chuckled again. "Well, it seems this Petticoat Lane was a paradise for pickpockets because it was always packed with people. Your grandfather told me that one Sunday he went up there with his cousin Jimmy and in the crowd they saw a man use a straight razor to slit another man's back pocket and as the man's wallet fell out, the thief caught it and disappeared into the crowd."

"Didn't the man know what was happening?"

"Oh no. These thieves were very clever at what they did, and the poor man would have had no idea he had lost his money until he felt in his back pocket. I remember though, your grandfather saying it taught him a lesson early and when he went back there as a grown-up he never carried a wallet in his back pocket."

"Was his grandfather really like that, Gran? Grandpa says he was known as a cunning old horse trader. Doesn't that mean he wasn't very honest?"

Jamie's grandmother smiled. "Well, I wouldn't go so far as that Jamie, but he did live by his wits much of the time. Still he did have a job, looking after the horses at a local brewery. He loved horses you know. Does your grandfather mention how he nearly got killed trying to save them when there was a fire at the brewery?"

"No Gran, he doesn't. What happened?" Jamie asked eagerly.

"Well, one night the brewery caught fire and before the fire brigade could get there, your great-great-grandfather, as he was, went into the stables and dragged about half the horses to safety; and you know enough about horses to know they can go crazy near a fire. How he did it, no one ever knew because these were those huge dray horses and he was a really small man."

All the way home Jamie tried to visualize the teeming

market called Petticoat Lane and that world of long ago but found it impossible. There was simply nothing like it in his hometown or anywhere else he had been, and there was certainly no one like the great-great-grandfather he had just heard about.

Back in his room after supper that night Jamie settled down with his grandfather's notebook, more eager than ever to find out what was going to happen next. What he found was a sudden and dramatic change in the story.

—◦◦◦—

"My dad says they got everything that can float over there."

We were huddled in our still unused shelter and for once even Puddy was subdued as we discussed the drama that was unfolding across the English Channel, at a place we had never even heard of until a few days ago.

For weeks now, we had listened to reports of the German army, smashing its way at will through Holland and Belgium, leaving the much vaunted Maginot Line standing useless, miles away from the real fighting and forcing the British expeditionary force closer and closer to that small coastal town that was forever to become a part of British history.

Now they were fighting for their very existence and the only thing left behind them was the sea.

"Do you think the Jerries will invade?"

Sammy's question seemed to rekindle Puddy's normal aggression.

"Bleedin' hope so. We'll give it to the bloody square heads if they try to land here."

"I heard my dad talking to your dad, Sammy, and he said there's nothing to stop the Germans now," my cousin Jimmy put in.

"Your dad don't know what he's talking about. Take more than Hitler and old fat guts Göring to beat us." Puddy glared at Jimmy.

Jimmy opened his mouth to say something else but took one look at Puddy's face and closed it again.

"Yeah, and with everyone joining the Home Guard, old Jerry'll wonder what hit him."

"Too bleedin' right, Danny." The look on Puddy's face left no room for further discussion on the subject.

"I'm going to join the Home Guard as soon as I'm sixteen. My Uncle John's already a corporal and he's going to get me in . . . you going to join, Puddy?"

"Nah, Charlie, too much spit and polish for me. I'm going in the Merchant. Be in early next year."

"I'm going for the Royal," Sammy piped up. "Battleships, that's for me."

"You'll never get in anywhere if you don't comb your bloody hair," Puddy said, and we all broke up laughing, for Sammy's uncontrollable hair was an endless joke.

"Well, there ain't no point in me deciding anything

because my dad said they won't let me go."

Puddy withered my cousin with a contemptuous look. "Yeah, well while you're hiding behind the apprenticeship your old man got you, we'll go and win the war for you."

"Me, I don't know," Danny said, "I think I'd like to be a pilot but it's tough to get in."

Danny was yet to find out that fate was going to deal him a safe hand and an unknown doctor was going to make his decision for him.

"See, I told you old Jerry can't beat us. Got the whole bleedin' army out, right under his stupid nose."

It was one week later and the miracle of Dunkirk was on everybody's lips. Puddy had his grinning face about one inch from my cousin Jimmy's nose as we huddled in the shelter.

"Yeah, well we ain't won yet, Puddy," Jimmy retorted with a boldness that surprised us all. "My dad says everyone is talking about invasion, and we'd better see what Churchill has to say before we get too excited."

Puddy's face went dark red. "Yeah, well one thing, Churchill won't bleedin' quit no matter what your old man says."

"Why don't we all meet at my house and see what he says," Danny put in quietly, pouring soothing oil on the argument. "My mum and dad will be next door and we can listen to Churchill on our wireless."

"Sure, why not," Puddy agreed, then swung back to my cousin, "still betcha Churchill won't quit though."

"Shh, here he is," Danny said, twiddling the tuning knob and volume. We all crowded closer to the set as that deep growly voice that we were all to draw so much inspiration from in the months and years ahead, came through the speaker:

"The battle for France is now over and I suspect the battle for Britain is about to begin. On its outcome rests the future of Christian civilization."

Puddy threw a triumphant glance at my cousin and started to speak. *"Shut up,"* we all hissed. Puddy glared but said no more.

"The whole fury and might of the enemy must soon be turned upon us, for Hitler knows he must break us in this island or lose the war. If we can stand up to him —"

Puddy could contain himself no longer and leered at my cousin, yelling "we're going to fight." The words from the radio cut through Puddy's shout, *"but if we fail, then the world will sink into the abyss of a new dark age."*

Now we all looked at each other and even Puddy stopped grinning. In spite of everything that had happened and my cousin's gloomy predictions passed on from my Uncle Jim, we had never really considered the possibility that we could lose this war, but here was our "saviour" accepting that very possibility.

The deep gravelly voice brought us back to the present.

"Let us therefore brace ourselves to our task and so conduct ourselves, that if the British Empire and its Commonwealth last for a thousand years, men will still say . . . this . . . was their finest hour."

We all just sat and looked at each other, the gravity and inspiration of those words overwhelming.

———

For the first time, Jamie could almost visualize a place he had never seen and a time he never knew. He read far into the night as he found himself caught up in his grandfather's story and the obviously titanic battle that took place all those years ago.

———

"What's your old man say now eh! Hundred and sixty Jerry planes shot down." Puddy stabbed at the newspaper with his finger and glared at Jimmy.

"Yeah, the Spits have got them scared stiff. They'll chuck it in by Christmas," laughed Sammy.

"Better bleedin' not," snarled Puddy. "I want a go at 'em yet."

"Me too," chorused both Danny and I.

"Well Crikey, so do I," said Sammy, "but my dad says if they keep losing planes like this, they'll have to quit."

"He means they'll have to quit bombing, not the bleedin' war, dummy."

The Battle of Britain had been raging for some time now and the fighter pilots had become our new heroes. Although we still went to the movies regularly, the Hollywood variety that we had grown up on had long since been pushed into the background with the emergence of these real live heroes.

"Hey, there's another story about that Canadian. Says he shot down three Jerries again." Puddy was pointing at another story on the front page which read:

CANADIAN ACE SCORES AGAIN
Willie McKnight, the young Canadian from Calgary, Alberta destroyed three enemy aircraft in a single sortie, the second time 242 squadron's ace has achieved this remarkable feat. Rumour has it this young hero is up for his second D.F.C.

Alongside the piece was a picture of a slim, dark young man in flying gear. He was smiling and his eyes had that same mischievous look I had come to know so well in my Uncle Dick.

Jamie stopped reading, a puzzled look on his face. How come we never hear about Canadians like this at school, he wondered. His thoughts flew back to a trip he had made to Calgary with his parents and grandparents a couple of years ago. "McKnight Boulevard was the name of the road we turned on to from the highway," he said out loud. "Could it have something to do with *this* McKnight?"

Then he remembered something else, voicing his thoughts aloud again. "Grandpa went to some airplane museum while we were there — I wonder? — grandma should know." He turned back to the story.

—◇◇◇—

"Isn't that guy something else," Danny said, a mixture of envy and pure adulation in his voice.

"Yeah, just imagine meeting him."

Willie McKnight epitomised these legendary heroes of the sky. He had flown in France throughout the battles there, his squadron taking a terrible beating, fighting a rear-guard action against overwhelming odds. It was in France he had earned his first Distinguished Flying Cross.

But it was not just us youngsters who hero-worshipped these young flyers. All the people of Britain had a blind faith in them to win this battle, even though it hung in the balance, right until the end.

Perhaps the strangest part of the Battle of Britain, which would eventually prove to be the pivotal battle of the whole war, was the fact that we saw very little of it, the fighting taking place high over the fields of the English countryside, between London and the coast. The reason for this was that it was a battle for supremacy in the air, for it had long become obvious to the military, that whoever controlled the skies would, in the end, win the war. So, although invisible to us, the whole country was aware of the importance of what was going on and followed the see-saw struggle through newspapers, radio and the newsreels in the cinemas.

Even so, it had an unreal quality about it, almost like the movies we kids loved, making it hard to grasp the reality of people dying, up in those summer skies.

"When I was down at my Gran's in Pitsea last weekend, one waved at me," I said, being deliberately obtuse about the story I had been dying to tell ever since we met in the shelter.

"One what?" said Puddy.

"A Spitfire pilot," I burst out, not being able to maintain the *blasé* act for more than the first few seconds. "He flew right over my Gran's bungalow. Bet he wasn't more than twenty feet up. There were bullet holes everywhere but he just grinned at me over the side of the cockpit and waved. He had this long white scarf on — just like John Wayne in 'The Flying Tigers.'"

Everyone's eyes were on me. Envy fought with disbelief. Puddy challenged the one part of my story he could.

"Come on Charlie, twenty feet — he had to be higher than that."

"Well, not much." I rushed on, not done with my story yet. "He crash-landed just over the hill, right by the Messerschmitt he had just shot down."

Now everyone's eyes were popping but Puddy, ever suspicious, said, "How do *you* know where he crashed?"

This was the moment I had been waiting for and I tossed in my *pièce de resistance.*

"Cause we went up and saw them. There was only one policeman there and although he wouldn't let us touch anything, he let us go right up and look."

Now the questions flew at me — "What'd they look like? did you see their guns? — was the Jerry dead?"

"Nah, the Jerry didn't die. The policeman said he baled out over Chelmsford. They caught him right away."

"Damn," said Puddy in disgust.

"What about the Spit pilot — was he hurt?"

"No way, Danny. Should have seen his plane though, like a bleedin' pepper pot."

———

"Gran, do you remember when we went to Calgary a couple of years ago?" Jamie was sitting in his grandmother's kitchen, munching on one of the cookies she had just baked.

"Yes." His grandmother looked puzzled.

"Didn't Grandpa go to some airplane museum while we were there?"

"That's right, why do you want to know?"

"Well, in his story, he talks about a fighter pilot from Calgary named McKnight who was quite famous and I remember we drove along a McKnight Boulevard, and I was wondering whether it had anything to do with him?" Jamie finished off his sentence hurriedly, thinking his idea now sounded a bit silly.

Far from laughing, his grandmother looked at him with a shrewd look.

"And you think this museum might know something about this young pilot?"

"Well — yes."

"Then let's go and look through your grandfather's things. If I know him at all, there will be a program or *something* tucked away."

"There, I knew it." Jamie looked up from the drawer he was looking through, to find his grandmother waving a sheet of paper. "It's called the Aerospace Museum and there's an address and phone number." She handed the paper to Jamie, a triumphant smile on her face.

"Gee Gran, thanks — thanks a lot."

"What are you going to do now?"

"Try to phone them, I guess — could I come here and do it, Gran. I'd kinda like to do this myself."

His grandmother gave a nod. "I think I understand. Come round when you like."

"Thanks again, Gran."

"You're welcome, Jamie. You know I'm kind of enjoying this myself."

Her words gave Jamie the encouragement to ask one more question. "Gran, who was Göring?"

His grandmother smiled. "Oh Göring was second in command to Hitler. As Commander of the German Air Force, he was the one who convinced Hitler that he could bomb us into defeat, so their invasion plans were put on hold, luckily for us," she said in a kind of grim tone.

Jamie looked up at his grandmother, realizing by her tone that his grandfather and friends had obviously been wildly optimistic about their chances of repelling an invasion, then, remembering his original question, he went on, "They seemed to think this Göring was a bit of a joke."

"Well, he was a bit of a show off and also very fat, so this made him a natural butt for jokes, but he had been quite a famous fighter pilot in the First World War, so I doubt men like Churchill took him so lightly."

Jamie shovelled his supper down that night, eager to get back to the story and see if there was any more about this Willie McKnight. His mother and father smiled approvingly, assuming he was doing homework. Closing his bedroom door, he flopped onto his bed, opening the notebook eagerly.

———

"Going to the Odeon this afternoon then, Charlie?"

"Yeah, soon as I have my dinner. Who else is going?"

"Sammy and me. Don't know about Puddy, says it's all kids' stuff. Just 'cause he's nearly sixteen, he thinks he's bleedin' superior."

"Aw, you know Puddy, Jimmy, I bet he'll turn up. He wouldn't want to miss his pie and mash."

Saturday afternoon at the movies followed by pie and mash at Mudie's was a ritual for us all. Mudie's Pie and Eel shop stood opposite the Odeon cinema and here, for fourpence, you could get a big meat pie and piles of mashed potatoes, smothered in gravy. What was in the meat pies now we were in a war, heaven knows, but this was *our* version of dinner at the Savoy. Most grown-ups would have the eels, that slithered around live in huge trays. The eels would be cut up to order and served in some sort of jelly.

Later that afternoon, as the three of us swung past Puddy's gate, Puddy came out.

"You going to that stupid picture then?"

"Yeah, coming?"

"Well I ain't got nothin' else to do — you going for pie and mash after?" We all smothered our grins.

"Course," I replied. "We always do, don't we."

"Might as well then. How's Danny?"

"He had his operation on Friday. It was a burst appendix."

"Think he'll still be able to join up?"

"Not very likely. According to my mum, there was complications."

"Geez, he ain't going to like that."

Puddy turned on Jimmy. "Well, at least he's got a real reason, not like some."

We had been stuffing ourselves with crisps, sweets and pop for about an hour, glorying in the exploits of the "Resistance" as they spread mayhem amongst the Germans, blowing up trains and stealing food while the Gestapo ran around in circles and Puddy, with all the maturity of his extra six months, kept muttering, "bloody stupid."

My bladder suddenly started sending out signals that it was overloaded, so I reluctantly left the "Resistance" planting dynamite under the Gestapo headquarters and went to dispose of my excess fluid.

There was a small window set in the wall above the urinal and I was gazing up at the sky, thinking what a beautiful day it was, just like that other September day one year ago when this war began when I saw them.

They covered the sky, the larger ones flying in strict formation and the smaller ones circling constantly. It looked as if all the birds had decided to migrate early, but I had already seen enough of war to know these were no feathered creatures.

I rushed out of the toilet, frantically trying to button my flies.

"Bombers . . . hundreds of 'em," was all I managed to blurt out, when, accompanied by a mighty roar, the head of the Gestapo chief was wiped from the screen and the cinema plunged into total darkness.

No one moved. It was as if they had been frozen in their seats. Then the second explosion rocked the cinema and, like puppets whose strings had all been jerked at the same time, everyone surged to their feet. But the cinema manager had already done his work. The exits were locked and an usherette stood guard at every one, their torches throwing murky beams through the dust-laden air.

The manager himself was on the stage, a torch in each hand.

"Now keep calm, everyone. You are all much safer here and 'arry's going to entertain you on the organ."

"Roll out the Barrel" started to drift up from the pit, where, during the interval of every performance, the organ, psychedelic lights flashing, would rise majestically from its resting place, the flashing lights turning Harry's white suit into a multicolour of purples, greens, reds and yellows.

So, for two bizarre hours, as the bombs rained down and the huge chandeliers swung madly, jingling out a crazy chorus of their own, we sat singing songs, accompanied by an invisible Harry, playing an invisible organ, both stuck firmly in the pit by the power failure. Each time another bomb fell and exploded outside, those chandeliers would look as if they were about to come crashing down on our heads and clouds of plaster dust would fall from the ornate ceilings, filling the air like smoke and covering everyone in a film of dirty white powder.

Suddenly it was over. Although Harry was still in full flight with "Knees up, Mother Brown" to which the sirens, sounding the "all clear", added their own mournful wail, yet paradoxically there was an eerie silence.

Slowly everyone got to their feet and filed from the cinema.

"Holy Mother of God," someone whispered. There was the same hushed stillness as in the cinema and the same sun was setting in that same serene blue sky but now it danced across a blanket of shattered glass, making it seem as if all the diamonds in the world had fallen from the heavens.

Trolley bus power cables writhed like angry snakes, jumping high into the air as they shorted against each other, sending cascades of sparks into the darkening sky. It was almost as if our Guy Fawkes night firework display had come early — until, that is, we looked around. Buildings that just a few hours ago had seemed so solid were now piles of smouldering rubble.

We turned our eyes toward Central London, where a wall of flame shot hundreds of feet into the air. It was then we started to run because our own street seemed ablaze from end to end.

"It's bleedin' Harrison Barbers," Puddy gasped as we reached the top of Bisson Road.

We collapsed in almost hysterical laughter as we saw he was right.

"Blimey, it stinks worse than ever."

"What do you expect, Sammy. There's ten tons of old bones and rats burning over there."

Harrison Barbers was a soap factory that stood on the

other side of the canal. In the yard were piles of bones from which marrow was taken and used in making soap.

These huge mounds were home to hundreds of rats, and every so often the exterminators were brought in to spray them. When this happened the piles would writhe like living things as the rats tried to escape the deadly poison.

The rats came from the canal and one of our favourite pastimes as kids was to take our dogs under the dank bridges and go rat hunting. I owned a little brown dog that was a cross between a thoroughbred pomeranium and the huge Chinese chow. He looked like a miniature chow and would fight with this breed's ferocious savagery. No rat, however big, was safe from his fury.

The stink Sammy was referring to was made when the bones were boiled to extract the marrow.

"What a bleedin' joke. Of all the places there is round here to to bomb, old Jerry hit that stinkhole. I reckon we ought to write to old fat guts Göring and thank him."

We all laughed at Puddy's joke but it was a brittle laugh, for in that short few hours on a beautiful September day in 1940, we all grew up a little, instinctively realizing that our world, as we knew it, disappeared that afternoon and would never return.

4

A Canadian Ace

Jamie stood motionless in front of his grandfather's grave, staring fixedly at the headstone. After some time, he bent down and absently plucked a dead flower from the vase that was standing on the grave.

He shook his head as if he were trying to clear it, then turned away, kicking idly at the loose gravel as he left the cemetery. Outside he hesitated for a moment, then, nodding to himself turned in the direction of his grandmother's house.

"I went to his grave on the way here."

His grandmother, who had been walking toward the kitchen spun around, her eyes filling with tears. She grabbed Jamie to her for a moment, holding him close. Jamie could smell the odor of fresh baking coming from her apron. She pulled away as quickly, rubbing her eyes and smiling.

"Like something to drink? I have some new cookies."

"Please, Gran." Jamie peeled off his coat and sat down as his grandmother went into the kitchen.

He sat looking around. Although he had been in this room many times, it was only now, today, that he really saw it.

There, on the large unit that stood against the wall were several pictures of himself, at various stages of growing up. He wrinkled his nose at the one of him standing naked in the yard. Above, there was one of his Aunt Deb, who taught at university. On another shelf was a picture of his mother and father and one of his Uncle Matt, who spent all his time abroad. In fact, Jamie had only seen him four times.

He got up and picked up the photo of his grandfather, then stood staring at it, as if he hoped it would speak.

"Here we are then."

Jamie nearly dropped the picture and put it back quickly, almost guiltily, on the shelf.

"That was a nice picture of your grandfather. I always liked that one."

His grandmother looked up from the table, where she was putting some hot chocolate and cookies.

"I have a feeling you're getting to know him quite well from that book," she said smiling. "Have you come to phone that museum?"

Jamie felt a deeper stab of guilt at her words, thinking

how little he had bothered to visit his grandparents before. In fact he had never been there without his parents until he had found the notebook.

"Well yes, Gran, but I *did* come to see you, too and talk about Grandpa."

For a moment his grandmother looked infinitely sad, then she smiled again. "I know dear and I'm glad. Now, let's try that number. I'm as curious as you are, to know about this young flyer."

Jamie dialed the number and a woman answered. He hesitated, not knowing quite what to say. His grandmother nudged him and whispered, "Just ask if they know of this McKnight?"

The woman's voice came back clear and full of enthusiasm. "Oh yes, we know all about Willie McKnight. We have a whole display devoted to him and we are restoring one of the original Hurricane fighters that he flew. Did you know that McKnight Boulevard is named in his honour?"

I was right, thought Jamie.

The woman was speaking again. "You should try and visit us, young man. The guide here will be able to tell you much more about him. He was, you know, one of our country's great heroes of the war."

"Thank you — thank you very much, ma-am. I intend to."

"You should go, Jamie," his grandmother said when Jamie told her what the woman had just told him. "Get your father to take you."

"*No,*" his grandmother was a bit surprised at Jamie's vehemence. "I just want to do this myself, Gran, I'll save the money to go."

His grandmother looked at Jamie for a moment, then touched his cheek lightly.

"If that's what you want, dear."

Back home that night before he started reading more of his grandfather's story, Jamie wondered why he was keeping this whole thing to himself. He still felt strongly about not showing it to his parents, although he was not really sure why. But he *could* have shown it to his friends. Tozer would have loved the bit about the girl, he thought with a smile. No, it was just a feeling he had had, right from the moment he first opened the notebook — a feeling that this story, somehow, was for him alone.

Shaking his head he started reading again.

———

"Did you hear about old Boney?" We were all wedged in one corner of the shelter, which was now full every night.

Although most people had the small steel "Anderson" shelters in their back yards, the German bombing was so consistent, that the only way anyone could socialize was to spend a couple of nights a week in the large street shelter.

"You mean Billy Bone — what's he done now?" Sammy answered as we all turned to Puddy, who had tossed out the cryptic question.

"He's a — hero, that's what." Puddy lowered his voice dramatically as he uttered the forbidden word, but in spite of Puddy's virtual whisper, old Mrs. Harris must have heard, for her head swung round sharply.

"'Ere, you watch your tongue, young Cecil, or I'll be 'aving a word with your mother."

We all kept our grins hidden, knowing Puddy's almost paranoid hatred of his real name.

"Boney, a bloody hero, that's a tall one, Puddy," my cousin said.

Billy Bone was one of seven children and lived in Abbey Lane, the next street to ours. The family was poor, even by the pre-war standards of the Depression years and no one had ever seen a Mr. Bone.

Billy, a couple of years older than all of us, had been in and out of Borstal ever since he left school.

"It's bleedin' true all the same," Puddy replied.

"What'd he do? Nip over to Germany and kick old 'Fat Guts' Göring in the arse?" Sammy laughed.

Puddy ignored Sammy's feeble attempt at humour.

"You remember that woman who was trapped with her kids in that burning house up the High Street."

"Yeah, someone pulled them all out and disappeared before anyone could find out who. Geez, that wasn't Boney?" All our mouths hung open as well as my cousin's, who had posed the question.

"Bleedin' was. The only way the coppers found out was

because when he got home all his hair was gone and his only jacket was burnt to bits so his mum give him hell, but young Dougie heard about the rescue and told the coppers — now they got to give him a bleedin' medal for bravery."

"Geez, what a laugh. The coppers giving Boney a medal. That I'd like to see."

"Wouldn't we all, Sammy," Puddy said.

"'Ere, what you doing. Get orf my bed," screamed a voice.

"Sorry missus, got to check the emergency exit." The man stepped across old Mrs. Harris's bedding and started climbing the steel ladder leading to the escape hatch in the roof.

Suddenly the hatch was flung open and a beam of light shot up into the night sky, making the shelter a perfect target for the bombers overhead.

For a few seconds there was total silence, then Puddy roared. "He's a — spy, let's get him."

"Get 'im Cecil," Mrs. Harris screamed, all concern at Puddy's language now forgotten, "get the dirty bleedin' traitor."

Puddy grabbed the man's legs and dragged him down from the ladder. Two men now arrived and joined in.

"Bleedin' traitor," they yelled, fists flailing.

By the time two special constables arrived from the shelter entrance the man was a bloody mess, his nose broken and his eyes swelling.

Puddy had already pulled the hatch shut and the Air Raid

Warden now climbed up and secured it with the bolts.

The incident kept the local gossip alive for weeks and the story of how we caught a spy lasted for years. In reality our "spy" was a member of the Irish Republican Army. Many of the people of Ireland supported the Nazis, if for no other reason than they hated the English. Still, as far as we were concerned he was a full blown spy and we had helped to catch him.

———

"Hey Jamie — wait up." Jamie looked round and groaned. Tozer was pounding up the street.

"You coming to ball practice this Saturday? We got a big game coming up against the Cougars week after."

"Don't know Tozer, might be busy."

"What's with you lately. Nobody ever sees you."

"Nothing, I just got something I have to finish first."

"Like what?"

"Nothing you'd be interested in. Hey, you remember that story about old Mr. Brannigan having a barn full of old war stuff — you think there's anything in it?"

Tozer was staring at Jamie open mouthed. "What the hell do you want to know about that for?"

"Never mind." Jamie turned and took off at a run, leaving an even more surprised Tozer staring after him.

Jamie had no idea why the Brannigan thing had popped into his head at that moment because, in spite of all he had been reading about the war, the story of the reclusive old farmer's supposed collection of war memorabilia had not entered his thoughts before he met Tozer.

Stories about Mr. Brannigan had been legion among the local kids for years. None of them had ever been on his farm because he did not exactly throw out the welcome mat and maintained only the most essential contact with local tradespeople, so it was virtually a given that the children would make up stories about him. But the rumour about his barnful of war relics had long been a part of adult gossip, too.

"You seem to be spending a lot of time indoors these days, Jamie." Although his mother's voice was enquiring, it also had a hint of pleasure in it.

"Got a special project I'm working on," Jamie answered, satisfied that he was not telling a lie.

His mother beamed. "Well that's good, Jamie. I'll let you get on with it then."

Jamie breathed a sigh of relief and shot upstairs to his bedroom. But before getting out his grandfather's notebook, his thoughts returned again to old Mr. Brannigan. "Sure like to get a look in that barn," he muttered. Then he picked up the notebook and started reading again.

—⁓—

"Hi Jimmy."

"Hi Charlie, where you going?"

"Got to take this plaster of Paris up to a dentist in Ilford."

"Heard you got a new job. What's it like?"

"It's O.K. I get out a lot. This is the only thing I don't like though." I hefted the package containing four bags of plaster back under my arm. "This stuff's bleedin' heavy. How come you're not at work though?"

"I'm on nights this week. What a game. Every time we get started, old Jerry comes over and we have to bolt for the shelter."

"Yeah, know what you mean. Sometimes it takes hours to deliver one thing but as my boss says, a war don't stop some guy from needing his false teeth — *quick the bank!*"

We both dived head first into the entrance of Barclays Bank as the machine gun bullets started spraying the street. Almost at once the anti-aircraft guns started their staccato barking and bits of shrapnel from their shells started pinging off the pavement like giant hailstones.

As quickly as it had begun, the raid was over and apart from the continuous wail of the "all clear" siren, everything was quiet again.

These "one off" lightning raids continued all through the war and their sheer unpredictability made them, in many ways, worse than the actual Blitz of London. Several years later, I was to find out first hand how destructive they could also be.

"Bloody hell." I was looking at my parcel of plaster which lay split open and scattered all over the bank entrance floor.

"Blimey, now I'll have to go back and pack another one and I'm late already. Better run, see you Jimmy."

"See you Charlie," my cousin yelled after my rapidly departing back.

—⁓—

Gee, fancy having to go to work like that, Jamie mused, looking up from the book. Wonder if they still went to school?

—⁓—

Shoving the fresh parcel at me my boss pushed me out of the door. "Hurry up now, they are still waiting for this."

Sprinting for the bus stop, I jumped on a trolleybus just as it was pulling away and, dumping my parcel under the stairs, I raced to the top and along to the front seat. We swung around Stratford Broadway Church and passed the boarded-up windows of J.R. Roberts store, where I had worked until recently. I glanced across at that blank facade, knowing that in spite of its battered look, "business as usual" was going on behind those plywood sheets. The church was on a concrete island in the middle of the road and Stratford High Street split at this juncture, one road going left to Leyton and Leytonstone, the other swinging right to Manor Park and Ilford.

As the trolleybus approached the traffic lights at Manor Park Broadway, it suddenly slowed to a crawl. A bus was lying on its side. It was peppered with bullet holes and the ambulance workers were bringing people out of the wreckage.

I looked at the number of the bus. It was the one I had just missed, when I had met up with my cousin.

Jamie sat quietly staring at the book. He was thinking how close it came to never being written and how easily he might never have known his grandfather at all, or — the thought struck him with a shock — not even have been there himself. He felt tired and knew he should go to sleep but couldn't stop reading.

"Your Uncle Dick was injured last night. He's in hospital." My mother's voice was tight with emotion.

I dropped the fork with which I had been shoveling down my supper, eager to get to the shelter and brag about my miraculous escape to the gang.

"What happened?"

"An incendiary bomb hit him while he was fighting a fire."

A picture of the deadly fire created by these bombs flashed into my head.

"Is it bad, mum?"

"I don't know too much but his arm's all smashed up and badly burned. Your Aunt Maisie's the only one allowed in to see him at the moment."

Pictures and sounds of Christmases past flashed across my mind, pictures and sounds of laughter, of my Uncle Dick banging away on his drums as the kids danced in the snow outside our window. Suddenly, the anticipation of seeing the look on the gang's faces when I recounted my adventures of the day faded and I didn't go to the shelter that night after all.

When I finally did see my Uncle Dick, all the love of life had gone from his eyes and I never heard him laugh again.

"Guess what," I couldn't keep the bragging tone from my voice, "my brother's going to be a pilot."

"Oh, the lucky sod," Danny's voice was wistful.

"Yeah, he's already been accepted and just has to get his release from the Red Cross."

"Will they let him go? I thought that was a reserved occupation?"

"It is, Danny, but my brother said they need flyers more and the Red Cross will have to let him go. Don't think my mum's too pleased though, what with my Uncle Dick and all."

"*What* do you mean, your Uncle Dick? What's *happened* to him?"

With the excitement of my news, I had forgotten until Sammy spoke that I hadn't been to the shelter the last two nights.

"He's in hospital. An incendiary bomb hit him and smashed his arm up."

"Oh no. How bad is it?"

"Bad enough, Puddy, but we really don't know much 'cause my Aunt Maisie's the only one allowed in to see him."

"Geez, what a week. Jimmy told us about you two being shot up in the High Street the other day." Puddy's voice actually had a touch of admiration in it, which was really surprising considering he was talking about my cousin as well as me.

His words, although unexpected, nevertheless brought back all the happenings of that day and the other tale I had to tell.

"Yeah, what he didn't know, though, was the bus I missed just before the raid started was shot to bleedin' pieces up at Manor Park. I saw them bringing out the people when I went past. Looked a right soddin' mess — bodies everywhere." I felt very smug as I embellished my tale, for everyone was hanging onto every word.

Jamie woke to the sound of his mother's voice calling from downstairs. His grandfather's notebook lay open on the bed and his reading light burned palely against the sun pouring through the window.

"Jamie, hurry up or you'll be late for school."

Jamie looked at his bedside clock. It read a quarter to eight. He flew out of bed and, dragging on his clothes, ran downstairs, combing his hair with his fingers as he went.

He was in trouble twice during classes that day as he kept nodding off, but still, come that night he could not stop himself picking up the notebook again.

—⁓—

"You see this?" Danny had a newspaper in his hand and he was pointing to the section that listed all the decorations due to be presented by the King at Buckingham Palace.

Puddy craned forward and read the list. "Hey that guy McKnight is getting his second D.F.C. tomorrow."

"Yeah, presented by the King."

"Another Distinguished Flying Cross. Wow, he must be good," said Sammy.

"Gee, I'd like to see that," I put in.

"Well, that's what I was thinking. How about we go up there and see?"

"Hah, you won't see nothin'," Puddy snorted at Danny.

"Maybe not much, Puddy, but we might see him coming out. Anyway, I'm going. Anyone else like to?"

"Sure, I would." Sammy ran his hand through his hair.

"Me too," my cousin said.

"Well, if you want to, I might as well. Bet we won't see nothin' though," said Puddy, having the last word as usual.

We were up at Buckingham Palace early the next day and

had ourselves wedged right up against the railings by the time the presentations began on the lawn.

"Told you, we wouldn't see nothin'."

For once we all had to agree Puddy was right, for the ceremony was so far away, all we could see were vague figures standing in a row. Periodically, each one would step forward to where the King was and he would pin on the medals but we had no idea who they were, or what was being said.

"Come on, let's go do something." Puddy was getting irritated.

But Danny wasn't ready to give up yet. "Wait a bit, they've still got to *leave* ain't they, so we could still see McKnight."

"Blimey, that'll take forever."

"Don't matter," said Sammy, "we ain't got nothing else to do."

"O.K, O.K., but I still think we're wasting our time."

It did seem like hours we stood near the gates of the palace, watching the people milling around talking but eventually the ceremony ended and everyone started to leave.

"He's there, look, right there!" Danny was jumping up and down with excitement.

We all craned forward and there, in the midst of a group of airmen, was this small, slim, dark-haired man, laughing and gesticulating to the others. On his chest we could see his D.F.C. with the shiny new bar, denoting his second medal, hanging below it.

"See, I told you, didn't I?" Danny was triumphant.

Suddenly a beautiful girl, in the uniform of a Woman's Army Corps officer appeared from the crowd and took his arm, leading him to a sports car, parked nearby.

"Wow, did you see that?" Sammy's voice was dripping with envy.

———

Jamie's thoughts turned to the trip to Calgary that he now almost had enough money for. "Maybe I know some things about this guy that they don't," he mused. Suddenly catching a glimpse of his bedside clock, Jamie reluctantly closed the notebook.

Tomorrow was Saturday and there was something he had to do.

5

Mr. Brannigan's Barn

That Saturday dawned sunny and clear and Jamie was up early, evoking an enquiring look from his mother.

"Where are you off to so early?" she asked, as, shovelling down the remains of his breakfast, Jamie jumped up and grabbed his coat.

"Just going for a ride, maybe see some of the gang." Jamie's answer was only half the truth.

"Well don't be late back for your lunch."

"No. I won't, mum." Jamie shot out of the door before she could say any more and grabbed his bike from the garage.

"Should be safe for a couple of hours," Jamie puffed as he pedalled furiously along the road out of town, "old Brannigan is usually in town for the morning."

Reaching the entrance to the farm, he hid his bike in the hedge and peered across to the Brannigan farmhouse.

"No sign of his truck. Good, he must have left already."

Jamie slipped through the hedge and across the field. There were two large barns located some distance behind the house, one much older than the other and it was this one Jamie headed for.

"Bound to be in there," he said to himself.

As he reached the large doors, he groaned. There was a large padlock and chain securing them.

"Well, you idiot, what did you expect?" he castigated himself.

He walked slowly down one side of the barn, his spirits dropping when he saw there didn't appear to be any other way in. But as he got to the rear of the building, his spirits soared again. High up in the wall there was a window and lying on the ground, a rickety old ladder, half buried in the grass. Jamie tugged it free. Several of the rungs were missing and it wobbled precariously. But, determined to make the most of his luck, Jamie propped it against the wall and climbed carefully up to the window. Rubbing away the grime with his sleeve, he peered through. It was gloomy inside but gradually he began to make out some shapes.

So, it *was* true, he thought excitedly, for down on the ground, he could see what looked like a cannon of some sort and alongside it, a couple of what he was sure were machine guns. Towards the front of the barn were a number of what appeared to be pieces of broken machinery, mixed up with metal frames.

"Wonder what all that stuff is? Looks like junk to me."

He lifted his foot to climb another rung, hoping to see better. It was one of the missing rungs.

Jamie opened his eyes and looked up into the stern, unsmiling face of Mr. Brannigan.

"So, you're awake."

Jamie swivelled his eyes around and took in the unfamiliar room, then brought them back to the old farmer.

"What did you think you were doing, young man? You could have killed yourself."

Jamie stuttered, "I'm sorry, Mr. Brannigan. I only wanted to see if you really had some old war stuff in your barn."

"What'd you want to know that for?"

"Well, you see, sir. I've got this notebook that belonged to my grandfather and it's all about the war and it got me interested and so I wanted to have a look . . ." Jamie's voice trailed off and he looked anxiously at the farmer.

Then Mr. Brannigan surprised him totally. "Well, you could have just asked, instead of trespassing on my property and almost breaking your fool neck."

"I'm really sorry, sir. I should not have done that. You won't tell my parents, sir, will you?"

The old farmer surprised Jamie even more by giving him

a crooked grin. "Well, I guess it's no worse than I did myself at your age. I could tell them, I suppose, that you fell off your bike and I found you."

"Gee, thanks Mr. Brannigan. I'd better go now."

"Oh no, lad. That's a nasty bump you have on your head and you might have some concussion. I'll take you home and your parents can get you to the hospital."

Jamie suddenly became aware that his head ached. Reaching up he touched the sore spot. There was a large bump there.

"Come on, lad, let's get you home and when you are feeling better, just come back legally and I'll show you the stuff in the barn, if you're still interested."

Jamie could hardly believe his luck. "Gee thanks again, Mr. Brannigan. I'd really like that."

Mr. Brannigan helped him up and taking him out to his truck lifted Jamie up into the passenger side and strapped him in.

"Now just sit quiet while I get you home."

"Yes, sir." Jamie was actually quite happy to sit back and close his eyes, for the effort of getting out to the truck had made him feel dizzy and he realized that Mr. Brannigan was probably right about the knock he had taken.

Mr. Brannigan stopped to pick up Jamie's bike on the way out and put it in the back of the truck. He then headed back to town.

Jamie's parents were in a state of panic by the time Mr. Brannigan brought his truck to a stop outside their house.

They both rushed out to the truck when they saw Jamie climbing out.

"Oh Jamie, what happened — where have you been?" His mother was close to tears.

Jamie looked across anxiously at Mr. Brannigan, fearful that he might decide to tell his parents the truth, but the old farmer was as good as his word and repeated the story of Jamie falling off his bike.

"You should get a doctor to look at his head. He has a nasty bump there." Giving Jamie's parents barely time to blurt out their thanks, Mr. Brannigan unloaded Jamie's bike, climbed back into his truck and was gone.

A visit to the hospital revealed that Jamie, apart from the bump and a mild concussion, was apparently none the worse for his accident. But, for safety, his parents were told to keep him in bed for the next twenty-four hours.

Lying in bed, Jamie still couldn't believe his luck. "Gee, fancy old Brannigan being like that. Guess we were all wrong about him," he said to himself.

His forced confinement allowed him a real opportunity to get back into his grandfather's story and he eagerly fetched the notebook from the cupboard where he kept it hidden, opening it at the place he had marked.

—∿∿—

It was in November of 1940 that my mother's nerves finally cracked under the incessant bombing and my father took her to my grandmother's home in Pitsea. Because of work and my Home Guard duties, it was arranged for me to stay with my Aunt Mabel and Uncle John in Leytonstone and it was January of 1941 before I found time to go back to my old street to see if I could find any of the gang.

"Blimey, if you don't do something with that bleedin' bayonet, you're going to castrate yourself."

I hitched up the oversized army belt and swung the bayonet from between my legs for the tenth time. Puddy was leaning on his gate, a large grin plastered across his face. He looked very grown up in his navy-blue seaman's jersey.

I walked carefully across the street. "Got to get my Aunt Mabel to shorten it. So you're in then?"

"Yeah, been signed up for a while now. Just waiting for my first ship. Where you living now, then?"

"I'm staying with my Uncle John and Aunt Mabel up at Leytonstone, 'cause it's too far for me to come up from Pitsea. I have to be on call now I'm in the Home Guard." I spoke with what I hoped was a sense of importance.

"How'd you get in then. I thought you had to be sixteen?"

"You do, but my Uncle John's a sergeant now and signs up all the new recruits, so he fiddled it."

"Pity he couldn't fiddle you a uniform that fitted." Puddy eyed my baggy uniform with a sarcastic smile on his face.

I ignored the sarcasm. "Is Jimmy home?"

"Don't know. You going round to show off then?"

I bridled at the remark that was very close to the truth, for a little showing off was just what I had in mind.

"Course not. I just haven't seen any of you for a while, so I thought I'd come down and see if anyone's around. What about Sammy or Danny?"

"Saw Sammy 'bout an hour ago, don't know about Danny though. Where's your rifle then, or are you supposed to charge in and de-gut the Jerries?"

"Course I got a rifle but I don't carry it around everywhere; it's at my uncle's."

"So they ain't making you supply your own pitchforks any more then?"

"Course not. That was only in the beginning. We got lots of weapons now."

"Yeah, like what?"

"We got mortars and grenades, and we got Browning machine guns — *they're American*," I said with a touch of superiority.

—␣␣—

"Wonder if Mr. Brannigan's got one of those," Jamie mused, "be great if he has." He returned to the story.

—␣␣—

"Bet they don't let you fire them. Bet you ain't even got bullets for your rifle," Puddy sneered. "Yeah, well that's where you're bleedin' wrong, Puddy. When I do guard duty outside our headquarters, I have a clip in the gun and one up the spout and . . ."

"Geez, I must remember not to walk past there then. I might get my ears shot off."

"Next week we are going down to the range and practise with the machine guns," I finished breathlessly, determined not to be put down.

"Hey, here comes Sammy."

"Blimey, Charlie, where'd you get that uniform? Looks as if it would fit Fatty Arbuckle." Sammy had come to a halt, a large grin on his face and was running his hands through his unruly hair.

"Better watch it, Sammy. He's got a gun at home and might shoot you." Both were now laughing fit to bust and I realized my triumphant return was not going at all as I had envisaged.

"Yeah, well you might laugh, but old Jerry might still invade and you'll be glad of us then."

"*Crikey*, I hope not," Puddy chortled. "*I hope not.*"

"Yeah, well we'll see. Anyway I gotta go." I stormed off, with Puddy and Sammy's laughter following me down the street.

I hurried on down to my Aunt Kate, knowing it was close to tea time and war or no war, my aunt still made great cakes.

My cousin, I found out, was on the night shift and what

would have been disappointment an hour ago now turned to relief as I sat down with just my Aunt Kate.

Although I felt sure there was the hint of a smile in my aunt's eyes, she showed no other sign of mirth and when she put a pile of toast, jam and some of her cakes in front of me, I began to feel much better.

"If you like, I'll shorten that belt for you after tea."

"Thanks, Aunt Kate. I was going to ask Aunt Mabel to-night but it is kind of a nuisance." I looked at my aunt with almost slavelike gratitude.

"I heard you were staying with John and Mabel. How is your mum since she moved to Pitsea?"

"Better, I think." I grabbed a cake and took a bite. "But I don't think dad's too happy, though. He has to get up at five and walk along the railway tracks to get to the station. The other day he tripped and lost his false teeth. Took him and grandad ages to find them."

Aunt Kate chuckled. "I can imagine Henry not being too amused. Still it was for the best. Lillian was quite shook up after that bomb hit Mrs. Blake's house."

"Yeah, that was close. I remember we all thought it was our house when the bomb fell."

"I'm not surprised. After all, Mrs. Blake's place was right behind you."

As our houses only had a small backyard, the bomb had landed literally right behind us and I remember clearly the clatter of (as we later discovered) bricks, roof tiles, windows and doors as they rained down on our Anderson shelter. In fact, we had spent the whole night convinced it would be our house we would find in a pile of rubble the next morning but it turned out our only damage was the loss of our old parrot who had died, presumably, from shock.

"Yeah, we sure got a surprise when we got out of the shelter the next morning and could see right through to their street."

"Must be hard on Mrs. Blake, what with her husband away and a six-year-old daughter to look after."

I mumbled some sort of reply through another mouthful of cake, having little grasp of the difficulties faced by a young mother whose husband was thousands of miles away in a jungle somewhere.

When I left my Aunt Kate's, my uniform still threatened to fall off, but the belt now fitted snugly and the bayonet swung smartly at my side.

Unfortunately, there was no sign of Puddy or Sammy, so I decided to head back to Leytonstone. I was just about to jump on a trolleybus when I heard someone yelling at me. I turned and there was Danny running toward me waving something in his hand.

Letting the bus go, I turned back. "Hi Danny, what's up?"

Danny looked very upset. "Take a look at this." He thrust the crumpled newspaper under my nose.

The headlines leapt from the page.

CANADIAN ACE MISSING IN ACTION

Willie McKnight, the legendary ace of 242 squadron was reported missing in action today. Douglas Bader, his squadron commander said McKnight and another Canadian, Flying Officer Latta, took off just after lunch on a routine "mosquito" patrol. These patrols consist of flying over the coast of France and harassing the German defences. The losses from these sorties has proved so minimal that most flyers treat them as an afternoon of fun. Today, however, McKnight and Latta must have run into something much more than expected for neither man has returned and both have been listed as missing in action.

"Oh hell. Puddy and Sammy obviously don't know, 'cause I saw them a little while ago."

"No, I wouldn't think so. I just got the paper myself."

"Let's go find them then, Danny."

We both turned back down Bisson Road and knocked on Puddy's door.

"Hah, see your aunt fixed it so your trousers don't fall down." Puddy was looking at my belt, a wide grin on his face.

Danny silently shoved the newspaper at him.

"Sod, what a crock." Puddy looked up from the paper, anger in his eyes.

It was the following Wednesday before Jamie's parents decided his head was O.K. and allowed him out, but during that whole time he had not looked at the notebook. He just could not bring himself to turn another page and fretted away in the house until he could get away on his own.

He knew now that he had to make the trip to Calgary and find out all he could about this Willie McKnight before he could go on with his grandfather's story, so the next three days were spent planning. His first visit was to his grandmother.

"Gran, I want to go to Calgary this Saturday but I don't think mum and dad will let me be away for so long" — here Jamie looked anxiously at his grandmother, for he had no idea how she would react to his request — "but they would let me come *here*."

His grandmother looked at him quietly for what seemed an eternity.

"How do you feel, Jamie?"

This was not what Jamie was expecting at all and for a few seconds he looked at his grandmother blankly.

"Your head dear — how's your head?"

"Oh, that's fine, Gran. The doctor says I am O.K. and no real damage was done."

There was another long pause. "If I didn't know how important this is to you, I would never agree to deceive your parents, Jamie, and I want you to know, I would not do it again."

Jamie rushed forward and hugged his grandmother. "Thanks, Gran, thanks a lot."

"What were you doing out at Mr. Brannigan's anyway?" Jamie's grandmother looked at him shrewdly, "Were you trying to get a look in his barn?"

Jamie looked up in astonishment at his grandmother. "How did you know?"

His grandmother smiled. "Well, most people, including your grandfather, knew about Mr. Brannigan's collection, so it wasn't that hard to guess what you might have been up to. Now, how did you *really* hurt your head?"

Jamie, once again surprised by his grandmother's insight, told her the whole story.

She smiled knowingly when he finished. "I would imagine he was completely surprised to find anyone, especially a young man, interested in his stuff. Most people aren't. So are you going back?"

"Oh yes, Gran, Mr. Brannigan invited me, so I am going as soon as I can after I get back from Calgary. I really want to see his collection."

"Good. I'm sure your grandfather would approve. Now, you had better get off home and organize your trip and don't forget to come and tell me all about it."

"I will, Gran, I promise." With that Jamie shot out of the door and ran home, full of excitement at the forthcoming trip.

6

The Aerospace Museum

A s the Alberta prairies rolled by the speeding bus on the two-hour journey from Red Deer, all Jamie's thoughts were focused on the notebook tucked in his pocket, still folded open at that fateful page. It had never occurred to him to ask the lady at the museum what had happened to the Calgary flier. It just seemed impossible that a pilot such as Willie McKnight would have been killed.

"Hello, young man."

Jamie knew from the voice that it was the woman he had spoken to on the telephone. She was plump and homely looking, just the opposite of his mother who was tall and rather thin.

Jamie found his voice. "I phoned you a few weeks ago about the flyer, Willie McKnight."

"Oh, I remember. I'm so glad you decided to make the trip, especially today because our curator is here and he can tell you more about Willie than anyone."

She called out and a slightly built man with glasses appeared.

"This is the young man who phoned about Willie McKnight. He has come to find out more about him."

"Well, let's take you round, shall we?" The man spoke with some sort of foreign accent that Jamie did not recognize, but he seemed friendly and led the way through a door behind the woman's desk.

It opened into a small room that was full of uniforms on dummies.

"This is Willie's dress uniform that his brother donated to the museum." Jamie stared at the uniform with its row of medal ribbons.

"It looks as if it would fit me," he said in surprise, staring closely at the small dress jacket and pants.

"Most fighter pilots were small. You'll see why in a moment."

The man then led the way through to the main hanger which was the museum's home for all the planes. Jamie gazed across the vast space. It was full of planes, some obviously from generations back, some from a much more modern era.

The curator walked over to where an area was enclosed by a large sheet hanging from the steel roof of the hanger. He waved Jamie behind the sheet into what was obviously used as a workshop.

It had benches all along one side where an assortment of tools lay scattered.

"This is a Hurricane fighter that we are rebuilding. It will carry Willie McKnight's personal logo. Did you know he had a large 'Grim Reaper' holding a scythe dripping blood painted on his plane? Seems characteristic from what I have heard of him. He was a bit of a lad, you know — only saved himself from expulsion at the University of Alberta by joining the Royal Air Force. But he was one heck of a pilot."

Jamie only half heard the words. He was staring at the frail looking thing that was the Hurricane standing over in the far corner of the workshop. Obviously still being restored, the plane had wings and wheels, but the fuselage was only a skeleton, consisting of a steel frame covered with (what the curator called) wooden stringers. This part of the plane, he went on to explain, would eventually be covered with a fabric the same as that already on the wings.

Jamie realized that all these men had had between them and death was their own skill and daring, for it was obvious once a hail of bullets struck the cockpit, they were almost certainly going to die. He was beginning to understand why they had been such heroes to his grandfather and all the people of Britain.

The curator was speaking again. "These holes on the wing edges are where the plane's machine guns would be fitted. The pilots had to be careful always to fire in short bursts because the guns fired so fast that all the ammunition could be used up in minutes. Even with care, they only had enough ammunition for about fifteen minutes; then they had to come down, re-arm and re-fuel. Later, the planes were modified so that some of the machine guns could be replaced with cannons. These cannons would fire small shells and were particularly effective for ground attacks.

"If you step up here," the curator was pointing to a set of short steps by the cockpit area, "you can see into the cockpit and you'll see what I mean about fighter pilots needing to be small."

Jamie, on looking into the cockpit, understood all too well what the curator meant. Only a very slightly built person could ever have got into the seat.

"The Hurricane, unlike its somewhat more famous brother, the Spitfire, could actually carry two people."

Jamie stared more than ever. There was some space behind the pilot's seat but he felt even he would have a struggle to get in there.

The controls, unlike those of the modern planes he had seen, seemed terribly crude, just bare metal levers and pedals.

"Didn't allow much for comfort did they," the curator grinned, somehow reading Jamie's thoughts.

"Will it fly when it's finished?"

"If we can locate the parts that are still missing, it will. This here," the curator was pointing to a huge engine sitting on the ground, "is an original Rolls Royce Merlin engine that was fitted into a wartime Hurricane. It has been overhauled and will go into the plane."

"What's still missing then?"

"Well, our main headache is the control dials for the cockpit. Everytime we find another plane, they are either missing or smashed beyond repair. Have you ever seen a picture of McKnight?" The curator walked over to a large blown-up photograph that was hanging on the wall behind the plane. It showed a group of fliers in front of what was obviously another Hurricane fighter.

"No, is that him?" Jamie pointed to the man standing in the centre of the group.

"No, that's Douglas Bader, the Squadron Leader. He had no legs, you know. Flew with artificial ones. This is Willie." The curator pointed to the man sitting on the wing of the plane, and as soon as Jamie looked at him, his grandfather's description came vividly to life. For there was the grin and the mischievous eyes.

After studying the photograph for a while, Jamie pointed back to the Squadron Leader. "How could he fly a fighter with artificial legs?"

The curator smiled. "I've often asked myself that question, but fly them he did and became one of Britain's most famous flyers, although at the time of this picture, Willie was the squadron's ace."

"How many planes did he shoot down?"

"Well, reports of pilot 'kills' as they called them were always difficult to assess and the officials would usually err on the cautious side so Willie's official total was, I believe, seventeen but Bader credited him with 21 and that's what's on the commemorative plaque at the airport. But you know it's not so much the number of planes that Willie destroyed that made him so remarkable but rather the short time he did it in. His war lasted barely a year."

"There's a *plaque* at the airport?"

"Oh yes. It was put there when the new airport was opened. Bader came over from England and officially unveiled it. It was all part of a campaign over several years that was spearheaded by him to force the city to recognize their most famous hero. In the end they were persuaded to name the boulevard after him and then the plaque was put at the airport."

"Do you know much about how he died? In my grandfather's story, it says he was on what was called a mosquito patrol and they were supposed to be easy."

"There's nothing easy in war, Jamie, and while it's true that, compared to what these fliers had done in the Battle of Britain, these patrols were much less risky, they could still be dangerous. The loss of Willie and the man he was flying with, prove that well enough."

"So, how *did* they die?"

"To this day, no one really knows. Both of them simply vanished."

"Didn't they find their planes or anything?"

"No, nothing. Which suggests they both went down in the English Channel, but there were no reports that day of any planes seen crashing into the sea. On the other hand, some pilots flying over France that afternoon, swore they saw Willie's plane chasing a German fighter some miles inland."

"So, there's no grave or anything?"

"No. I guess in some way, his grave is the plaque at the airport."

"Did you know him?"

"No. He was before my time, but I know quite a lot about him."

"Like what?"

"Well, Willie was definitely a rebel who found his cause. He seemed to delight in challenging authority and absolutely thrived on danger. I've heard stories of how he borrowed — borrowed being a generous description — his father's car to impress some girls and draped it over a neighbour's fence. Another time, he was driving his brother's car from Cochrane and gave another young man a lift. The story is that the man was so terrified, he could not stand when they got to Calgary and had to be carried from the car."

Jamie felt sure he would have liked Willie McKnight.

"What happened to him at the University?"

The curator chuckled. "Oh that. I understand he led a snake dance through the streets of Edmonton and snarled up the traffic for hours."

"And that was why he was expelled?"

"Well, he wasn't actually expelled, but he was on the brink of it, probably for many other pranks as well. Anyway, it was just about this time that the people from the Royal Air Force in England came around looking for volunteers to train as pilots and Willie jumped at the chance, probably as much because of his girlfriend as the threat of expulsion."

"He had a girlfriend here then?" Jamie was thinking of the English girl his grandfather had mentioned at the Buckingham Palace ceremony.

"Oh, indeed. I understand that she was the local Calgary beauty and every boy wanted to date her, but Willie wanted her all to himself, so they fought a lot, something you'll most likely go through in a few more years."

"How could he be such a good pilot if he was always in trouble?"

"Good question. According to the people who trained him and some of his own letters home, he was in as much trouble in the Air Force as he was back home, but I think the answer came from his flight instructor who said that Willie was a natural."

"A natural what?"

"Oh sorry. There are some people who have a gift for doing things and Willie was this way with planes. He just instinctively knew what to do. Even in the early days in France, long before they knew much about modern air combat, Willie was getting remarkable results."

Jamie remembered his grandfather's reference to France but he wanted to know more, so he didn't comment.

The curator continued, "242, of course was still an all-Canadian squadron when it was chosen as one of the few modern fighter squadrons sent over when the real war started in the spring of 1940."

"All-Canadian?"

The curator looked down at Jamie. "I see you don't know much about that part."

"Not really. I only know the bits about Willie McKnight that I read."

"Oh, O.K. then. I'll give you some background. 242 squadron was the first all-Canadian squadron formed in the war. It was made up of many of those pilots like Willie, who had been recruited by the Royal Air Force and gone over to England in the early days."

"You said it went to France?"

"Yes. You see, although the British had a good number of squadrons in France, the planes were all outdated and slow, so when the Germans started their offensive, it soon became obvious that the British planes were totally outclassed. In fact, they were nothing more than clay pigeons to the German pilots, so a decision was made to send over a few modern squadrons to try to stem the tide."

"Why did they only send a few then?"

"Ah, this was the great dilemma of the British. They knew that if France fell, the next phase of the war would be an attack on Britain and knowing, as they now did, that air supremacy would be the key to victory or defeat, they were stuck with a 'Hobson's Choice'. They could commit most of their modern planes to France and gamble that they could turn the tide, but then, if they failed, Britain would be at the mercy of the Germans.

"Alternatively, they could accept that France was lost anyway and keep those planes at home for the battle that would inevitably follow. The problem with that was that it would seem to the French that Britain was deserting them totally if they didn't do something, so a compromise was agreed on and they sent what squadrons they felt could be spared without seriously harming their capability to take on the Germans later. They chose only Hurricane squadrons for the operation because its production was well ahead of the Spitfire at that stage, and 242 was one of those squadrons."

"Is that where Willie got his first DFC? I read he had two."

"Yes, as I said, he proved very quickly that he was a nat-ural born pilot. I believe he shot down his first German plane within a day of getting there and within a month he did something he would repeat twice more. He shot down three Germans in one sortie."

"Was that special then?"

"Oh yes. As I said, those guns used their ammunition up very quickly so to destroy three planes in one action, a pilot had to be very good indeed. I heard that if the British pilots couldn't remember his name, they would refer to him as that flinty-eyed little deadshot from Calgary. Not that his name remained unknown for long. I understand that by the time the Dunkirk evacuation took place, he was the talk of every R.A.F. mess."

"You said 242 squadron was all-Canadian. That means Douglas Bader was Canadian too?"

"No, Bader was English. He took over the squadron when they returned from France the second time. This was because they had lost so many pilots, there simply weren't enough Canadians left to bring the squadron back up to strength, so British pilots were drafted in. Also, their origi-nal Squadron Leader — a man named Gobiel — was very sick and had to be sent home to Canada, so Douglas came in. Mind you, it was a blessing in disguise because Bader turned 242 into one of the top squadrons in the Battle of Britain."

"You said the second time the squadron came back from

France. Why did they go back?"

"Most people today think that the war in Europe ended after the British troops were evacuated from Dunkirk, but in fact the French fought on for some weeks and so Churchill, still feeling guilty about appearing to abandon the French, sent a number of those Hurricane squadrons back to help out again. I guess it seemed logical to use the ones that already had experience of the fighting there and so 242 was chosen to return with several of the other squadrons who had been there before."

Jamie was silent for a while, trying to digest all he had heard, but by now he was totally caught up in what the curator had been telling him and was determined to learn as much as possible while he was here. Also there was another question that had been hovering at the back of his head for some time.

"Why was the Spitfire more famous? Was it a better plane?"

"In some ways, yes. It was faster than the Hurricane but the Spitfire's biggest advantage over all other fighters, including the German planes, was in its manoeuvrability. It could turn faster and tighter."

"Why was that an advantage?"

"Well, it meant that if it had an enemy plane on its tail, it could turn inside the German and, from being the attacked, quickly become the attacker, like so." The curator demonstrated with his hands.

"You said it was only better in some ways."

"Yes, that's true. Its disadvantage was that, unlike the Hurricane its body was made of a fine metal. This meant it would suffer more damage from enemy fire, whereas many of the bullets fired at the Hurricane would simply go right through the fabric, doing little damage. Many people though, including pilots, claim the Hurricane's biggest advantage was in the fact that all its eight machine guns were set close into the fuselage so the firepower was more concentrated. That meant they would strike the enemy plane in one spot. In the Spitfire, however, the guns were spaced further apart so they would spray the enemy with a spread of bullets. This meant that while it might hit more of the enemy plane, it most likely wouldn't do as much serious damage. It's rather like the difference between a shotgun firing buckshot instead of shells."

Jamie stood silent trying to imagine those planes wheeling and diving around the sky, their eight machine guns spraying death and destruction at each other.

The curator broke into his thoughts. "As the war progressed and the Allies went more on the offensive, the Hurricane proved it had other advantages."

"What were they?"

"It proved easy to convert to a fighter bomber and also it could fly in virtually any weather. Because of these two factors, it went on to serve in every theatre of war, even on the Russian front. In Burma, it was said to be the only plane that could fly in a monsoon."

"How important *was* the Battle of Britain?"

"Oh very. Many historians, and that includes me, consider it to have been the most important battle of the whole war."

"Why is that?"

"Because as I said before, both sides knew that, unlike the First World War, supremacy in the air was going to be the key to victory, not only in each battle but in the whole war, and as Hitler had to defeat Britain to have any hope of final victory, the outcome of the air battle was crucial. Thank God for us all that he lost."

"Why couldn't Hitler win unless he beat Britain?"

"Well, if you look at a map of that part of the world, you will see that Britain was the only jumping-off place for an invasion of Europe. Take that away and Hitler's European fortress was untouchable. Even the Americans with all their power could not have launched an invasion without having Britain there to launch it from."

"Could the British have lost to the Germans?"

"Oh, I think it was quite possible. If you read up on the Battle of Britain, you will find that at one point, the fighter airfields were so badly damaged that their whole defence system was in danger of collapse."

"So, how did they win then?"

"I think there were two reasons. The first was undoubtedly the pilots. They achieved results that no one, especially the Germans, could have ever expected."

"What was the second?"

"That one is down to Hitler," the curator replied with a chuckle.

"Hitler?"

"Yes, you see, just as he had the British fighter defence in such trouble, he switched his bombing to London. Some say it was because he was enraged the British bombed Berlin in retaliation for a few bombs that had been dropped on London. Others claim it was a conscious decision helped by Göring's insistence that he could bomb Britain into defeat and so avoid their having to mount a full scale invasion.

Whatever the reason, one Saturday afternoon in September he sent a huge wave of bombers over to attack London, and, that, of course was the beginning of the London Blitz."

These last words brought back to Jamie his grandfather's story about that Saturday afternoon and the blitz that followed. He wondered what might have been, had his grandfather and all the British people not had such an unshakeable belief in their capability to beat the Germans, even though it seemed almost crazy.

"What time is your bus back?"

Jamie came to with a start at the curator's words and looked at his watch. He could not believe he had been at the museum so long.

"Gosh, I have to go." Thanking the curator and the receptionist, he flew out the door and headed for his bus.

7

Sticky Bombs and Hurricanes

Jamie sat on the bus, staring out of the window, endless pictures rushing through his mind. He barely stirred all the way home, his mind full of all he had heard that day.

Later that night, when he picked up the notebook and started reading again, everything was different. Before, he had felt just a spectator to everything that had happened all those years ago, but now as he read, it was as if he were back there, walking right alongside his grandfather as the story continued to unfold.

I released the trigger of the Browning machine gun and sat up, peering anxiously down the range to where the targets were. Suddenly, the coloured disc attached to a pole appeared and settled right over the centre of the target.

"Is that mine?" I asked the guy who was feeding the ammunition belt.

Before he could answer, I felt a tap on my shoulder. "Fire another burst, son," the sergeant said.

"Yes, Sarge." I settled down again and tucked my cheek against the pistol grip of the Browning. Squinting carefully along the sight, I lined up the gun and clamped it tight. Then, trying hard to breathe gently, I squeezed the trigger.

The machine gun shuddered as the staccato rattle shattered the air. Once again I sat up, watching the target. Up came the disc and settled right over the bull's-eye.

"O.K. son, that'll do. Come over here."

I got up and stood to attention in front of the sergeant.

"Where'd you learn to shoot like that?"

"Don't know, Sarge. I only ever shot an air gun at the fair. Did pretty good though," I added lamely, not knowing what else to say.

"Well, you've certainly got an eye for it."

Half an hour later we had all finished shooting and had broken for lunch.

"Hear you're our Sergeant York," my Uncle John grinned at me.

My chest swelled because I had seen the movie about the legendary American sharpshooter from the first war.

"Sergeant asked me where I learned to shoot."

"Well, he's already reported it to Captain Blain and you have just been made number one machine gunner as of now. When we go down to our defence positions this weekend, that's your job."

Crikey, I thought, why couldn't we have done this *last* weekend before I went back to our street.

After lunch we were all marched over to the grenade-throwing practice area.

"Right, gather round you lot," the sergeant bawled at us. He had in his hand what appeared to be a giant firework. It had a cylinder shaped top and a wooden handle. The cylinder appeared to be wrapped in some sort of shiny paper.

"Now pay attention. This 'ere is what they call a sticky bomb. The idea is that it will stick to a tank and blow a nice big hole in it. Underneath this paper is a very powerful glue, and the bomb can be used in two ways. Either you can run alongside the tank and plonk it on a strategic spot or you can toss it and it will stick where it lands. Either way, it won't do the tank a lot of good.

"For today we are just going to practise throwing at those boards which are supposed to be advancing tanks, now watch carefully as I demonstrate."

"Bet you a tanner I can throw it further than anyone." Billy Briggs was a hulking lad and undoubtedly one of the strongest in our whole company, so no one jumped in to accept his challenge.

"Let's each bet a penny," someone eventually whispered

from behind.

"Shut your yacking and pay attention." The sergeant carefully removed the wax paper and revealed a yellowy brown glue that looked something like that used on fly catcher strips, only much thicker.

"Now, I remove the firing pin, holding the detonator with my finger, just as we do with the ordinary grenade. Got it?"

Everyone nodded in unison.

"Right, now we toss the bomb, like so." The sergeant held the sticky bomb clear and deftly tossed it at one of the plywood sheets scattered around the field. The bomb stuck fast and exploded with a roar, blowing the sheet to pieces.

"Right, who's going first?"

"Me, Sarge." Billy Briggs looked at the rest of us with a grin.

"Penny each then, right."

Everyone nodded and he stepped forward, obviously determined to kill off the opposition with the first throw.

"O.K., now remember what I told you and don't remove the pin until you take the paper off."

We all watched eagerly as Billy peeled off the wax paper and drew out the firing pin, holding the detonator trigger down with his finger.

Then he turned toward the furthest sheet of plywood but, determined to put in a big throw, he didn't just lob the bomb but flung his arm back over his shoulder.

"Soddin' hell."

The sergeant went white, for Billy was standing there, his arm back over his shoulder and the bomb stuck fast to his back.

"Don't let go that pin for God's sake."

Billy looked terrified.

Captain Blain heard the commotion and hurried over.

"Oh God. Now keep calm, lad, and we'll soon get you free."

"I'm getting a cramp, sir."

"You'll get more than a bloody cramp if you let go of that pin," muttered the sergeant.

"Anybody got a sharp knife?"

Someone passed a large scout's penknife to the Captain.

"Now hold still, lad."

Captain Blain tried to cut the thick serge of Billy's battle-dress but it soon became obvious that his hacking could shake Billy's hand free.

"We need some scissors, Sergeant. Get someone over to the range office on the double."

No one needed any urging and two men set off at a dead run for the office, which was at least half a mile away.

"My arm's going dead, Sir."

"If you let go that frigging pin, it won't be just your arm that'll be dead," hissed the sergeant.

After what seemed an eternity, the two men reappeared with a large pair of scissors. Captain Blain carefully cut around the grenade and Billy flung it away.

"HIT THE DECK," the sergeant roared.

Billy's arm had been so numb that the grenade had hit the ground just a few yards away.

Clods of earth and grass flew into the air and showered all over us as we lay there pushing our faces into the mud.

All further practice was cancelled for the day and we were marched back to the trucks that had brought us to the range.

"You owe us a penny each, Billy."

"No I don't. No one else threw."

"Blimey, *anyone* could have thrown further than that."

Joey Smith was the one who had suggested we all bet a penny, and fright or no fright he wanted paying.

"Yeah but no one else did . . . 'sides, I could have been killed."

"What's that got to do with it, you bleedin' near killed us all."

"Aw, let it go Joey." Someone spoke from the other end of the truck.

"Still think he should pay," Joey grumbled, but said no more.

―⁓―

Jamie looked up from the book, speaking his thoughts aloud, "Geez, they talk about it as if it were baseball or something. Wonder if Mr. Brannigan knows about these weapons?"

Jamie arrived at Mr. Brannigan's farm and tossed his bike aside breathlessly, but the breathlessness was due as much to excited anticipation as his exertions.

Mr. Brannigan had been as good as his word, inviting Jamie out to his farm on the Saturday afternoon following Jamie's phone call.

The old farmer had the door open before Jamie could knock.

"Come along then, lad, we might as well go straight over." He strode away toward the barn, a large bunch of keys dangling from his hand.

He led Jamie to a smaller door on the far side of the barn that Jamie hadn't noticed on his previous visit. The door creaked loudly as Mr. Brannigan pushed it open.

"Don't get out here much now," he said by way of explanation, as he reached off to his left.

The barn was flooded with light as a dozen large old floodlights came on, creating artificial sunbeams through the dusty air.

Mr. Brannigan led the way to the far end, where Jamie had seen the machine guns.

"This one here is a British Vickers machine gun and the other is an American Browning."

Jamie's eyes focused immediately on the American machine gun. Walking slowly over, he knelt and ran his hands over the barrel, then grasped the wooden cased pistol grip of the gun. The gun itself was mounted on a huge tripod that looked enormously heavy.

"My grandfather talks about using one of these when he was in the Home Guard."

"Yes, the Americans sent a lot of this kind of equipment over, long before they got into the war themselves."

"The first time he used it, my grandfather said he shot the bull's-eye out twice at the range and they made him the No.1 Gunner." Jamie was surprised at the pride in his voice.

"Your grandfather must have been quite a shot to have done that. How did he learn to shoot?"

"Well, actually, he said it was the first time he had ever fired a gun. He was only fifteen then."

"Well, he had to have had a hell of an eye. He died recently, didn't he?"

"Yes. That's how I got the book. My gran let me have it."

"Read it well, son. That part of our history is being forgotten far too easily these days."

Jamie looked up quickly at the old man, surprised at the sad tone in his voice.

"Mr. Brannigan. Have you ever heard of a sticky bomb?"

"Told you about those, did he? Yes, they were quite effective against tanks. The guys soon learned that if you stuck one right on the track, it would blow it off and the tank couldn't move. Here's some ordinary grenades over here."

Jamie looked up on the wall the farmer pointed at. Fastened on it were numerous small metal objects, mostly either round or oval in shape.

"Don't have a sticky bomb though," Mr. Brannigan finished.

Alongside the grenades, a number of rifles and pistols were hanging.

"See this one, it's a German Luger. Picked that up in Europe in 1945."

"You were a *soldier* then, Mr. Brannigan?"

"Just an old footslogger — nothing special. Come down here and have a look at these."

These were the metal frames that Jamie had spotted just before he fell, but now, with his new-found knowledge, he realized what they were. He walked slowly around the nearest one peering at it intently and running his hands over the metal.

"Picked that one up from one of those dealers who sell wartime equipment and weapons. That was all that was left when I found it. He'd sold the engine and wheels and he said the fabric and wood had rotted away. From the look of it, it must have been lying in his yard for years."

Jamie turned around and spoke. "This is a *Hurricane,* isn't it, Mr. Brannigan?"

"How the devil did you know that?"

"Saw one a little while ago at the Aerospace museum in Calgary."

"You like to go to war museums then?"

"Well, not until now. It was something my grandfather wrote about, this famous fighter pilot from Calgary."

"Willie McKnight," the farmer broke in.

"Yes sir, that's him. They have a whole display down there and a Hurricane they are restoring, which is going to have his special markings when it's finished."

"Hm, knew about the boulevard and the plaque but I didn't know they had a Hurricane down there. Is it going to be able to fly?"

"Yes. That is they hope so."

"Aren't they sure?"

"Well, they have everything, including an engine but the curator there said there's some parts they still haven't found, mainly the cockpit dials."

"Hm." The farmer was staring up at the cockpit.

"Does *your* plane have them, Mr. Brannigan?" The idea flashed into Jamie's head so suddenly that he blurted out the words without thinking.

The farmer turned back quickly. "No–no, it doesn't."

Jamie suddenly felt the old man was not telling him the truth.

"Gee, wouldn't it be great if you helped them to make that plane fly, Mr. Brannigan."

"I told you my plane doesn't have any dials."

Although he didn't know why, Jamie realized he had trodden in forbidden territory.

"Sorry, Mr. Brannigan. I merely meant it would be great if you could have done."

The old farmer seemed mollified and his voice dropped back to its normal soft growl. "That's O.K., now let's forget it. Want some tea?"

"Well sure, thanks." Jamie was still finding it hard to come to terms with the fact that the man he and his friends had woven so many stories about was just an ordinary, nice old person.

Back at the farmhouse, Mr. Brannigan put a large kettle on the range and, digging into a cupboard, brought out a tin of biscuits.

"Here, help yourself while I get the tea made."

With the old farmer's parting words still ringing in his ears, "Some time, I'd like to read that book of yours," Jamie thought about his visit as he pedalled home. He still found it hard to believe the welcome he had received and Mr. Brannigan's genuine interest in his grandfather's story. But all this was tempered with the sure knowledge that sitting in that old Hurricane frame were the dials the Aerospace museum needed so badly.

I wonder why he doesn't want to give them up, he thought as he puffed up a steep hill, must be something important because he was real nice until I said that.

Jamie stopped as he reached the top of the hill and paused, staring back down at the farm. "Wish I could do something to change his mind," he said aloud, "but if I try and he gets angry again, I may never be able to go back there."

He sighed. "Gee, it would have been great to have those dials for the museum. Grandpa would have been pleased. Oh well."

Jamie shrugged and remounted his bike, then set off down the hill, the wind whistling in his ears as the bike gathered speed.

Jamie picked up his grandfather's notebook and started reading, but his disappointment over Mr. Brannigan's refusal to talk about the dials for the Hurricane kept intruding and it wasn't made any easier by a particular part of the story he was about to read.

—⁓—

"Blimey, this is bloody heavy." I heaved the 45-lb. Browning machine gun onto my shoulder.

"Ha, you should try this," Joey Smith shot back. Joey and three others each had one leg of the large tripod across their shoulders.

Billy Briggs was carrying two boxes of ammunition on his shoulder as easily as if they were empty cardboard boxes.

"You look like bloody coffin carriers," he laughed at the four.

—*∿*—

Jamie paused in his reading, "Yeah, I bet it was heavy," he muttered, a picture of the gun he had seen in Mr. Brannigan's barn flashing back into his mind.

—*∿*—

"Right you lot, let's get this stuff on the trucks. We are due away at twenty-one-hundred," the sergeant barked.

We loaded our gear and piled into the six Bedford army trucks that were parked outside our headquarters in Leytonstone.

Soon we were bowling along through the night to our defence line in Epping Forest. Earlier Captain Blain had given us our briefing for the weekend.

"This, men, is going to be a major exercise for us. The regulars are sending trained troops against our line. They will represent an invading force and it will be our job to stop them.

"Let me tell you now, those guys are going to use every trick they know to breach our lines. They won't want to be the losers in this — but *then* neither will we, so I want you all to be on your toes and alert to everything. If a leaf moves, you report it — *understand*?"

"Hey Briggsey, hope they didn't issue you with any sticky bombs, otherwise this'll be over before it starts." There was loud laughter from the back of the truck.

"Shut your mouth or I'll shut it for you."

"Quiet," hissed the sergeant, "or I'll shut both your mouths."

We left the trucks at the staging point and, loaded with our equipment, marched off to our defence positions.

"Sod." One of my crew carrying the tripod stumbled and fell to his knees. The darkness in the forest was total and the path we were on was only about eighteen inches wide. The sergeant turned and gestured angrily at us to be quiet. Suddenly the moon appeared and glinted on barbed wire just ahead. Soon we were all gratefully dropping our loads to the ground. There were slit trenches every few yards with sandbagged pillboxes in between. We were ordered to set up in the far left pillbox.

"Bloody boring, ain't it." It was now close to one o'clock and Billy Briggs had mouthed what we were all feeling. We had been peering through the bunker slit at the trees some twenty yards away for three hours and, apart from a few jittery moments earlier, when the moon shone on a bush or a breeze disturbed the trees, nothing had moved out there.

"WHO GOES THERE?" We all jumped about three feet in the air, as Joey yelled out the challenge, aiming his rifle at the bunker entrance.

"Quiet you fool, you want to tell the whole bloody German army where you are?"

"Aw Sarge, there ain't no Jerries out there."

"*Oh*, you got a special arrangement with Hitler then, have you Smith. What's he going to do, send you a post card? Or is he going to give you a ring on his private line? If so, do let me know when he calls."

Joey decided not to reply.

"Now listen up, you lot, supper'll be coming up shortly and I don't want you all sitting down as if it's a picnic. One stays on watch all the time. *Got it.*"

"Got it, Sarge."

"Right." The sergeant turned away then paused at the bunker entrance. "Oh, by the way, nice to see you were all awake."

Joey was eating his beef stew, standing at the slit. "Something out there," he hissed suddenly.

We all dropped our billy cans and crowded round the slit.

"Where? I can't see nothin'."

"Right there, by that big bush, something moved."

"You sure?"

"Come on, Billy, we all know Joey can see better in the dark than anyone. Let's get set up."

I settled down behind the Browning and Billy squatted by the ammo box. The belt with the blank cartridges was already loaded into the gun.

"I'll go and report to Sarge." Joey scuttled outside.

"Here they come."

About fifteen soldiers suddenly appeared out of the trees, running and yelling like maniacs. I set the sight on the left of the group and squeezed the trigger, slowly traversing the gun from left to right. The noise in the bunker was deafening as the gun spat out its blank shells.

Suddenly, a white armed marshall stood up and yelled at the men.

"O.K., you are all dead. I don't know whose firing that gun but he had you all in the first ten yards."

"Yea, we got 'em Charlie — we got the lot," Billy yelled.

"Hold on," yelled Joey, now back in the bunker, "we ain't done yet."

Another group had burst from the trees but this time they split into two, coming at us from both the left and right. I had to go for one and went for the right group, once again traversing the gun slowly from left to right and once again the marshall popped up, signalling them out of the battle but the others were coming fast now.

Billy suddenly shot up and out of the bunker. Crouching low he pitched his dummy grenade but this time he made no mistake. It landed smack in the middle of the charging group.

Once more the Marshall shot up. "Right you're out, you've just been blown to bits."

Billy came dancing back into the bunker. "Got 'em, right in the bleedin' middle."

Two more waves came at us before the battle was over but we managed to hold firm and repel them all.

The sergeant appeared at the bunker entrance. "Right lads, you can pack up now, the war's over for tonight."

"How did we do, Sarge?"

"The honours were about even. They broke through in the middle but both flanks held fast and we were able to counter attack and close the hole."

"Hey, right on eh, Sarge." Billy had a large grin on his face.

The sergeant smiled. "You lot did O.K. Got everyone they slung at you."

We were all tired but happy as we trudged back through the forest. All we wanted was a cup of tea and to climb into those trucks. The cooks were standing by with urns of hot tea as we got back to the staging area.

"Where's the trucks, Sarge?" We were all standing around sipping tea and feeling pretty smug.

"Oh, didn't I tell you. The enemy shelled our transport area. We have to walk home."

"But it's ten miles, Sarge, and what are we going to do with our gear?"

"That's war, son. You never know what's going to happen. As for your gear, you are going to carry it."

It was on that march back that I discovered the other side of being a machine gunner.

—⁓—

Jamie closed the notebook and thought about the machine gun he had seen that day. "Geez, how could they have carried that thing, it must have weighed a ton. And for ten miles — that would be sixteen kilometres."

In his dreams that night Jamie kept seeing a group of dials that seemed to be floating around his room but every time he tried to grab them, they burst, like soap bubbles.

"So, what happened at the museum?" Jamie's grandmother looked at him, her eyes full of curiosity as she put down the tray. She had not heard yet about his trip to Calgary.

Jamie related everything he had heard about Willie Mc-Knight while his grandmother sat silent, following every word.

"It sounds to me as if this young flyer and the many others there must be like him are people we should all know more about."

"That's what I thought, Gran. We never hear about Canadians like this at school."

"More's the pity, I say. Here have your drink and a cookie."

Jamie and his grandmother sat silent for several more

minutes, just sipping their drinks and nibbling at her homemade cookies.

"Gran, what was this Home Guard that grandad belonged to? I remember him saying something about it earlier in the story."

Jamie's grandmother came to with a start. "Oh yes, the Home Guard. Well, Churchill first started it after the fall of France, when an invasion was imminent. It was supposed to be a volunteer army that would help defend us against the German landings, not," his grandmother smiled, "that it could have achieved much at that time. The early volunteers barely had a gun between them and the ones from the countryside actually trained with pitchforks."

"What was the good of it then, Gran?"

"Well, most people felt afterwards that all Churchill had in mind was to give a morale boost to the public when we were in the worst situation of the whole war. After all, with France gone, we were the only country left in western Europe that Hitler didn't control and with the Russians having signed a peace pact with Germany, no one could help us at that moment."

"But Grandpa talks about machine guns and bombs and everything."

"Oh yes, that's true. With American help, the Home Guard very quickly became a well equipped second army and they were able to take over many duties from regular soldiers who could then be sent into battles elsewhere."

"But they were not much older than me."

"Not all, Jamie. The Home Guard was actually a mixture of very young men and older veterans, many of whom had fought in the First World War. So although it's true the ones like your grandfather were very young, they had a lot of experienced men guiding them."

"I went back to Mr. Brannigan's and he showed me all round his collection."

"Ah, I wondered why you hadn't been round before. What does he have in that old barn of his?"

"He has a Browning machine gun just like the one Grandpa used."

"Does he now. Your grandfather never knew that, I'm sure, otherwise he would have been round there himself."

"He also has the frame of a Hurricane there. I recognized it from seeing the one at the museum."

"How interesting. I wonder where he got it from?"

"He said he bought it from some dealer."

"Did he say why he buys all that stuff?"

"Not really. He just said he didn't want it to be destroyed. Did you know he was in the army, Gran?"

"Yes, I had heard. I suppose, thinking about it, that's really why he collects that stuff." Jamie's grandmother seemed lost in thought.

"Why *does* he collect it Gran?"

"Well, you know Jamie, in spite of all its horror, going over there to fight that war was, to many, the greatest adventure of their lives — and the friendships they formed have stayed with them even until today. I guess they went through things together that most of us never experience and that's why they can never quite forget the war or the people they went through it with."

"Gran?" Jamie hesitated, not sure whether he should bring it up.

"What, dear?"

"I think Mr. Brannigan's Hurricane has the dials that the Aerospace people need for their plane."

"And?" Jamie's grandmother was looking at him shrewdly.

"He won't talk about them. He just pretended the plane doesn't have any. But I *know* it does Gran, just the way he looked at it when I mentioned them."

"Did you ask him outright?"

"No, I didn't like to, but when I said how great it would be if he could help their plane fly, he got angry and shouted that his plane didn't have any, then insisted I forget about it."

"Well, it seems obvious you are right."

"Why won't he help, Gran?"

"I suspect Jamie, it's all to do with what I said about what they went through. That collection of his is the link to a time he can't, no, not can't, more likely doesn't want to forget."

"I guess then, there's nothing we can do."

"I guess not, Jamie."

8

The Home Guard in Action

That night as he continued reading his grandfather's story, Jamie felt more strongly than ever that he was no longer just a spectator but more like a time traveller transported to another world.

———

"Right, lad, remember the drill, one bullet up the spout but keep the safety catch on, don't want you shooting the locals."

I stuffed down the last of my fish and chips.

"Right, Sarge," I mumbled from a full mouth as I picked up my rifle and slipped in the clip of ammunition, then pulling back the firing bolt, I slammed it forward pushing a live cartridge into the breech. Slipping on the safety catch, I left the drill hall and took up my sentry position outside.

Very soon, the regular nightly wail of air raid sirens began and the heavy drone of bombers filled the night air.

Bet they're going to have another go at Three Mills, I thought. The Three Mills railway goods yard sprawled between Leytonstone and Stratford and the tracks ran just behind our headquarters. Three Mills was the major railway junction into London from the East and all rail traffic had to come through there.

Not surprisingly, the Germans had been trying to put it out of action since the early days of the London Blitz. Many people believed this was their target on that very first bombing raid back in 1940. Yet, like some targets that should have been easy to hit, Three Mills bore a charmed life, and no matter what the Germans did, it always came out virtually unscathed.

As I gazed up into the night sky, the searchlights began probing the darkness and the crunch of anti-aircraft guns filled the air. Suddenly, night turned into day as huge multiple flares fell from the bombers and lit up the sky. I watched fascinated. They looked like giant chandeliers (they were later called chandelier flares) and were obviously a new and dangerous weapon in the Germans' ongoing attempt to put the Three Mills yard out of action.

"Don't stand there gawping, lad, use your bloody rifle."

The sergeant had appeared beside me with four other men. They knelt quickly and took aim at the flares. I dropped beside them, released the safety catch on my rifle and squinted through the gunsight at one of the flares, which were now quite low.

We all fired together, the crackle of our rifles sharp and clear against the deeper crunch of the anti-aircraft guns.

"Got one," someone yelled as one flare broke up and fell to the ground.

We fired another volley and another flare went out.

"Down," yelled the sergeant, but we needed no bidding as the whistle of bombs mingled with the crackle of rifle fire. We all hit the pavement face down.

I don't know to this day whether the shooting of those flares had any real effect on the German bomb aimers but once again they missed their target.

We all got up slowly from the pavement. Fires were already lighting up the sky in Leyton and my old home area, just a few miles away.

"Looks like Leyton and Stratford are getting clobbered with incendiaries," muttered the sergeant.

"I think they got those bombs too, Sarge," someone said.

"Seems so." The sergeant turned back to me. "There might be another wave yet; next time, instead of star gazing, yell and start shooting if any more of those bloody flares come down. I'll send someone out with another clip of ammo. O.K., you lot, you can get back to bed for a while now." He gestured the men back inside and I was left with only the fires, the anti-aircraft gunfire and the occasional whine of bombs falling somewhere in Central London, for company.

"O.K. lad, on your feet."

I came awake with a start. "But Sarge, I just got off watch."

"That was two bloody hours ago. Anyway the A.R.P. and ambulance people are overloaded and need our help. Seems as if Jerry dumped his whole bleedin' load on Leyton and there's a hell of a bloody mess down there."

Two other men were already up and tugging on their boots. I quickly pulled mine on and laced them up.

"Let's go then — on the double." We ran out to the Bedford truck that was parked behind the drill hall and scrambled into the back with the sergeant already pulling away.

Leyton, which was just two miles from our headquarters, looked like Dante's inferno. Fires raged everywhere and rows of houses were reduced to rubble.

An A.R.P. warden rushed over. "Thank God, we need all the help we can get."

"Looks a right soddin' mess."

"This ain't nothing, Sarge. The shelter over by the traffic lights got a direct hit and a gas main burst. They reckon there's a couple of hundred people down there and we can't get in."

"Oh God," someone whispered.

"Where do you want us then?"

The warden jerked his head at one row of bombed houses. "We ain't even looked in there yet. Could you and your men work your way through and see if anyone's alive?"

"Leave it to us. Right, you two start at the other end, you son, come with me."

The sergeant and I clambered over the pile of rubble that was the first house and into what was left of it. There was no upstairs, but the kitchen and part of the living room was still standing. There was no one in the house.

"Must be in the shelter, Sarge."

"Lot of good that'll do the poor devils if they're in that one by the lights."

We worked our way through the houses until we came to the fourth one, located in the middle of the row.

This one was a little less damaged than the rest. Even part of the upstairs was still there.

"I'll check upstairs. You go through down here."

"Right, Sarge."

The sergeant climbed carefully up what was left of the staircase and I shoved the living room door aside.

I heard the whimper before I saw them.

A shard of glass was embedded in the woman's throat and her blood had trickled down over the baby's head.

—∿∿—

Jamie remembered those words as the ones that had caught his attention when he first picked up the notebook. Anxious to know what happened he quickly read on:

———

"Sarge, Sarge" — where the hell was the sergeant? Suddenly my vocal chords came unstuck and my screaming yells bounced off what was left of the walls.

"What is it, son? Oh hell." The sergeant who had rushed downstairs, stopped dead in the doorway for what seemed an eternity.

"O.K., let's get the baby out." He climbed across the smashed furniture and glass, then knelt down and prised the baby from its dead mother's arms.

The baby started to cry loudly now, his tears mixing with the drying blood from his mother's throat.

"Come on, son, let's get out of here."

I hadn't moved; my feet seemed glued to the floor.

"Come on then." The sergeant's yell woke me up and I moved towards the hole that had been the front door.

At that moment, my stomach heaved and half digested fish and chips flew over the wall and splattered on my shiny army boots.

———

Jamie paused for a moment, staring into space but it wasn't really space, for he was standing in that wrecked house, looking at a baby locked in its dead mother's arms, the smell of dust, blood and fish and chips filling his nostrils. After several minutes, he put the book aside and turned out the light. He lay for a long time staring at the darkened ceiling before sleep came and when he picked up the notebook the next night, it was with a mixture of compulsion and reluctance.

———

"Still guarding our shores from old Jerry then?" Puddy looked tanned but tired.

I did not react as once I might have done. Due to numerous tucks and take-ins, my uniform fitted me reasonably well now. I even got the occasional backward glance from a girl.

"Just got back then?"

"Yeah."

"Where'd you go?"

"Still on the New York run."

"How was it?"

"Soddin' rough. Old Jerry must have a couple of thousand U-boats out there. They pop up everywhere. Don't let you sleep for a minute."

I decided then and there not to mention my experience in the air raid on Leyton or anything else I had been doing. Somehow, there didn't seem any point.

"Heard anything of Sammy then, Puddy?"

"No, only that his ship's in the Med somewhere. They let you in a pub with that uniform on?"

"Oh sure, they don't turn anyone away in uniform anymore. Sammy's on the *Barham*, isn't he?"

"Yeah, so you want to go for a pint then?"

"O.K. by me, if you can find one the Yanks haven't taken over."

"Yeah, I had noticed. Blimey, there must be thousands of 'em."

"There are and they are not too popular with our guys. They got money coming out of their ears. What with that and silk stockings hanging out of their pockets, the girls are just falling over themselves to get a date. Our guys don't get much of a look in."

"Bet that causes some fun and games."

"Oh yeah, there's always a fight somewhere."

"Oh well, let them get on with it. All I want is a quiet pint somewhere."

"The Red Lion in Ilford's pretty good and we ain't seen too many Yanks in there. Bit too crummy I guess."

"O.K., how about we go to Mudie's, have some pie and mash, then jump a bus up to Ilford?"

"Sounds good to me. I can't believe it's still standing. There ain't nothin' either side of it."

"Yeah, bleedin amazing, ain't it. *And* the Odeon — both still there."

"Pity about the Empire though."

"Yeah, I heard it closed."

"I heard it was so badly damaged, it could fall down anytime. You know, Puddy, my dad used to take us all there every Saturday night. I saw Teddy Brown once and when we arrived, he was just getting out of his car. It was a huge yellow American thing and it had a special wide door, so he could get in and out. Blimey he was fat."

"Didn't know you ever went there."

"Oh yeah. From the time my dad got his good job, he took the whole family. We saw Gypsy Rose Lee once. Geez, was she ever something."

"You're kiddin'. They wouldn't have let you in there."

"Yes they did. There weren't no age limit in the theatre. You should have seen her, Puddy. Stark naked but she kept those big fans always in the right place. I remember screwing my neck all ways but never got more than a quick peep."

"I'd have liked to have seen that. Hey, do you remember the market?"

"Do I?"

"Remember how we used to split up and half of us would pelt down the road on our skates and scare the wits out of the stallholders, while the rest skated up the pavement and nicked a load of apples."

"Yeah, and I remember when you managed to catch a chicken one night."

"That's right, I did, didn't I."

The open air markets of those days sold everything, including meat and fowl, but because they had no refrigeration, the traders, at the end of the night would have to dump what they hadn't sold. So, what they would do was throw their leftover meat and chickens to the crowds. It was like a wedding bouquet ritual, only with food.

"Hey, you remember the fight between old Mosley's Blackshirts and the Jews."

"Blimey yeah, I had forgotten that, what a punch up."

Edward Mosley was a Fascist and Nazi sympathizer. He and his members all dressed like the Gestapo and because we were so near Bethnal Green and Whitechapel, home to thousands of Jewish people, his gangs were often in our part of London, stirring up trouble. On the night Puddy was talking about, around a hundred of them held a rally in the area of the market. Suddenly another group of men arrived.

Knowing the history of that time better now, I think they were more likely Communists than Jews because the Jewish people were not inclined to mob violence in those days. Anyway, a huge bloody battle erupted with about fifty police involved.

"Yeah, that was some fight. I remember one copper diving into the crowd with his truncheon and disappearing — wonder what happened to him?"

"I think there was more than one finished up in hospital. Let's go then, shall we?"

"Bloody hell, look at that." We were strolling up the High Street, looking at all the devastation, and had just drawn level with a hole where a house had been. Puddy was looking up and pointing. Up where the second floor had been, was now just a wall with a fireplace still attached to it, but it was not the fireplace Puddy was pointing at. Still hanging on the wall, by the fireplace, was a birdcage.

As we stared upward, there was a fluttering in the bottom of the cage, followed by the beautiful trilling notes of a canary.

"Holy cow, that bird's still alive." It was the first time I had ever heard Puddy express total surprise.

"Let's see if Mudie's got a ladder and get it down."

"O.K." We went on up the High Street to the pie and eel shop.

Mr. Mudie sent his son down with us and, with Puddy holding the ladder, I went up and unhooked the cage.

The bird panicked for a few seconds and started flapping around but I got it down safely and almost immediately it settled on its perch and started singing again.

"This place belonged to old Mrs. Blake. It was hit the night before last." Mr. Mudie's son suddenly spoke.

"Where is she then?"

"She's dead. They said she wouldn't go to a shelter. Her daughter was always round here, trying to get the old lady to move in with her but she was a stubborn old woman."

"Do you know where her daughter lives?"

"No, but my dad does."

"Best thing then is for him to take the bird and give it to her."

The canary, now fully recovered and still singing happily, was turned over to Mr. Mudie and we sat down to a pile of pie and mash.

"Where you lads going tonight?"

"Up to the Red Lion in Ilford for a pint."

"Well stick that money back in your pocket and have one on me." Mr. Mudie pushed the money we had given him for our supper back across the marble-topped counter.

"Gee thanks, Mr. Mudie."

"That's all right. I reckon old Mrs. Blake would have wanted me to do that. She loved that canary."

"That was a bit of alright Charlie, we can have an extra pint on that — 'ere have a coffin nail." We were sitting upstairs on the bus, our feet propped up on the window frame. Puddy pushed the familiar green paper pack of five Woodbine cigarettes at me. Woodbines were the cheapest cigarettes on the market, so we had all cut our teeth on them; so to speak. We drew on the cigarettes, puffing the foul-smelling smoke at the roof of the bus and feeling pretty good.

"Hey, let's go, Puddy." We clattered down the stairs and swung off the bus platform before it came to a stop at Ilford Broadway.

"What you 'aving Charlie?"

"Pint of brown." I was looking at the barman nervously because in spite of my bragging about being allowed in pubs, I had never tried it and was only going on what some of my Home Guard buddies had said. But he drew the two pints and, apart from a little smile, took no further notice.

"Bunch of Canucks down there, Charlie."

"Yeah," I looked at the group of Canadians drinking quietly at the other end of the bar, "they're O.K. They don't bother no one unless someone bothers them. I just hope no Yanks come in because if they start chucking their weight around, the fists are going to fly."

We were just on our second pint when the inevitable happened and a bunch of Americans, more than a little drunk, came crashing into the pub.

They pushed their way up to the bar, sprawling from one end, right up to where the Canadians were drinking.

"Hey watch it, you just spilt my beer."

"Well if you didn't take up so much room, I wouldn't spill it."

"Look, Yank, we are just having a quiet drink. Now why don't you just cool it and stay at your own end."

"Oh, you own that part of the bar, do you?" The American had his face about one inch from the Canadian soldier's nose.

"Oh-o, here it comes, Puddy." We were standing over by the window away from the bar area.

The Canadian shoved the American away and turned back to his drink, but the American grabbed his arm and spilled more of his beer. A huge fist smashed into the American's face, breaking his nose and spreading blood all over his face. Suddenly, all hell was let loose as fists, chairs and glasses started to fly.

In a few moments it was over and the Americans were all spread out on the floor.

"Geez, they never learn, Puddy. Those Canucks are bleedin' crazy. Nobody in their right mind messes with them, but the Yanks always have to stick their necks out."

"Must remember never to get on the wrong side of them — hell of a fight while it lasted though," Puddy had a big grin on his face.

At that moment, a bunch of Military Police burst into the bar.

"O.K, what happened?"

"It was the Yanks started it, Sergeant. Everything was fine 'til they came in."

The sergeant looked at the publican, then at the mess. "What about damages?"

"We'll take care of it." The Canadian who had first hit the American took a wad of notes out of his pocket. "Come on you lot, divvy up. How much do you reckon will cover it, sir?"

"Hey, how about that, eh! They reckoned our guys were a tough lot," Jamie grinned as he put down the book and turned off his light.

"Gran, what was the ARP?" Jamie asked the next day.

Jamie's grandmother put down her tea and smiled across at him. "That was the abbreviation for Air Raid Precautions and the people in the ARP were called Air Raid Wardens."

"According to Grandpa, they rescued people who were bombed."

"That's right. They rescued people and kept watch for where bombs fell and also made sure no one left their blackout curtains open at night when they had lights on."

"Blackout curtains?"

"Yes. Everyone had to line their curtains with black material so that no lights could be seen by the German flyers."

"In the bit I read last night, Grandpa talks about this guy Mosley and he says he was a Fascist and supported Hitler."

Jamie's grandmother's lips tightened. "Oh yes, Mr. Mosley caused a lot of trouble around where your Grandpa grew up."

"How could they let him do that, Gran?"

"Well Jamie, before the war, I'm sorry to say, there were a lot of people, some of them high officials, who felt that the British could make peace with Hitler. They refused to listen to Churchill and many branded him a war monger. Even several years into the war, some of them were still trying to undermine Churchill by pushing for a negotiated peace. Thank God, they never got their way or we would all have finished up in concentration camps and the Nazis would still be ruling Europe today."

Jamie was a little taken aback by the solemn tone of his grandmother's words.

"But the Americans would have beaten them in the end, wouldn't they?"

"Even the Americans could not have brought an invasion fleet across the Atlantic, Jamie, so it's hard to see how they could have."

Jamie realized his grandmother's words were an echo of what the curator of the museum had said and was again surprised that she seemed to have such a grasp of what went on all those years ago.

She suddenly seemed to return to the present and smiled in the way he was used to. "Anyway, young man, you had better get yourself home before your mother and father come looking for you."

"Thanks, Gran." Jamie shrugged on his coat and, with a hug from his grandmother, left.

That night, Jamie's mother discovered his badly neglected homework and he was forced under her watchful eye to do some overdue catching up. By the time he got to bed he was too tired to read, so he was reluctantly forced to wait until Saturday before he could get back to his grandfather's story.

It was raining again that day and with his mother and

father out shopping, Jamie was at last able to relax and open the notebook once more. The story had moved on yet again to another period.

—⁓—

By the early part of 1943, my mother and father had returned from Pitsea and we had just moved into a house in Ilford. It was here that I got first-hand experience of the sheer havoc a lightning raid could cause.

Around seven-thirty in the morning, I was in the kitchen with my mother, stuffing down a last piece of toast before leaving, and thinking I would go and see my cousin after work, when I heard a plane. Strolling to the back door, I yanked it open and had a look out —

"Get down, mum," I yelled as I myself fell back onto the floor. The plane was a Messerschmitt 110 fighter bomber and it was literally flying along the backyards of our houses. I had barely touched the floor when the bullets started to fly and a belated siren began to wail. My mother was under the table and we stayed glued to the floor until the plane flew past, its machine guns still chattering frantically.

This raid lasted only about ten minutes but when I finally took off for work the destruction was unbelievable. Roofs of houses were gone and glass was everywhere. A bus was jammed up against a lamp post, peppered with bullet holes. An ambulance was backed up to the bus and the attendants were busy bringing out passengers. I couldn't tell how many of them were alive but the driver was certainly not one of them. He lay slumped in his seat, his head smashed beyond recognition.

Later, on the news, we were told that just three planes had taken part in the raid and they had got through the radar unseen by flying at rooftop height, something I could attest to. The news also said that none of them made it back, even as far as the coast. But the most astonishing part of the news story was in the statement that those three planes, in the brief ten minutes the raid lasted, destroyed or damaged almost twelve hundred properties, killed thirty people and injured hundreds more.

Because of the chaos, I was able to finish work early that day, so I headed straight to Stratford. As I jumped off the bus the morning's events quickly faded when I first heard the newsboy yelling.

A wind was blowing and the large poster was flapping up off its stand, so I couldn't see it at first, then I picked up the words of the boy. "Barham sunk wiv all 'ands."

The poster settled down at that moment and there was the proof of what I had heard. *"H.M.S. Barham sunk with all hands."*

I quickly grabbed a newspaper and read the account.

The Battle Cruiser Barham received a direct hit from a torpedo yesterday. The missile struck the engine room, breaking the ship in half. No survivors have been located, and it is assumed they all went down with the ship which must have sunk within a few minutes.

I hurried on down to my Aunt Kate's house and it was obvious from her face that she already knew.

"How's Mr. and Mrs. Napthali taking it, Aunt Kate?"

"Hard. They knew last night. Someone came and saw them."

"Oh hell, poor old Sammy."

"That's not all, Charlie," my cousin now spoke up. "Puddy's missing."

"WHAT, how?"

"Well, all they know at present is his ship was hit on its way back from New York but no one knows whether he's alive or not."

"Oh crikey, what a day."

Tea was forgotten and it was another week before the Skittrels heard that Puddy had been killed in the explosion that sunk his ship.

9

The Hurricane Dials

"Holy cow," Jamie breathed, staring up at the ceiling, as he thought about Puddy's death at sea. He was jarred back to the present by the jangling of the phone. Putting the notebook away, he clattered downstairs and picked it up.

"Jamie."

"Gran, is anything wrong?"

"No, nothing. Are your mother and father out?"

"Yes Gran, they're shopping. Shall I get them to call you when they get in?"

"No, it's you I wanted. You'd better come round."

"What is it, Gran?" Jamie was mystified.

"You'll see, just come round."

"O.K."

Jamie shrugged on his coat and ran out of the door.

"Gran, what is it?" Jamie burst out as soon as he got in the door.

"See for yourself," his grandmother led the way into the kitchen and opening the back door pointed to the porch.

Jamie stepped past her. All that was on the porch was an old box. Jamie looked back puzzled.

"Look inside."

Jamie bent down and pulled open the lid. It was packed to the top with old newspapers.

He looked up at his grandmother. "I still don't . . ."

"Unpack it," his grandmother said.

Pulling the top layer of newspapers out, Jamie felt some bulky items wrapped in more newspaper. He lifted one out and was taken aback at its weight but this proved nothing compared to his astonishment at what was revealed when he unwrapped it.

Quickly, he pulled out the other packages and tore off the newspaper revealing the full set of aircraft dials.

He stood up slowly, one of the dials in his hands. "I can't believe it, Gran," he blurted out. "I wonder what made him change his mind."

"I can't imagine."

"Gran, I have to go and thank him." Jamie's voice was

now full of excitement as the meaning of the gift sank in.

"I think not. If Mr. Brannigan wanted you to thank him, he could have brought the dials to you."

"You mean he doesn't want me to go there?"

"Not at this time, Jamie. This was likely a difficult thing for him to do."

"But what about the museum? They'll want to thank him, won't they?"

"I think the same thing applies, Jamie. If he wanted their thanks, he could have given the dials to them himself, but he gave them to you."

"But what am I going to tell them? They might think I stole them."

"I doubt they would think you could find those things that easily after they have failed for so long. Are you going to take them to the museum yourself?"

"Oh yes, Gran — I *have* to."

"Well then, if they have any doubts about how you got them, you'd better tell them to contact me."

Jamie looked relieved and smiled his gratitude. Suddenly, a thought flashed into his head. "Gran, it's teachers' professional day on Monday. I could take them down then — oh, I can't, I don't have enough money for the fare." Just as quickly as it came, the excitement faded from his voice.

His grandmother smiled again and reached for her purse.

"No Gran, I can't."

"Oh, I think this is one occasion when it's justified, and I know your grandfather would approve." She pressed the money into his hand.

"Thanks, Gran, thanks a lot. Do you think Grandpa would be pleased?"

"I know he would. Now, there's one condition. You must tell your mother and father about all this. I can't justify deceiving them any more."

"O.K, Gran, I promise I'll tell them as soon as I get back from the museum."

"Good, I'll hold you to that, Jamie. Now, we'd better put that box somewhere safe until Monday."

Jamie watched anxiously as the bus driver stowed the box with the rest of the luggage in the compartment under the bus. Then he climbed the steps into the bus taking a final look back to be sure the luggage compartment was securely locked and found himself a seat on the same side.

It was not a relaxing journey, for every time the driver stopped to let a passenger off, Jamie would stand up and peer through the window to make sure the box was not being taken off the bus by mistake. He did not stop worrying until he had his precious cargo safely on his lap in the local bus that would take him to the museum.

"Hello, young man. I did not expect to see you again so soon."

The lady Jamie had seen before was staring curiously at the box he had deposited on the nearest seat with a sigh of relief.

"Is the curator in today?"

"Yes, he is, but at the moment is with the head of the museum. Can I help?"

"Well, not really, will he be long?"

"I don't know for sure, but I'll tell him you are here as soon as he comes out."

"Thank you, ma-am."

Jamie watched the clock ticking away on the wall. His precious time was disappearing and there was still no sign of the curator.

"Do you have to catch a bus home?" The woman had noticed Jamie's anxious glances.

"Yes, ma-am."

"Let me see if I can get through to him," she smiled, picking up the phone. She spoke for a few seconds and replaced the receiver.

"He'll only be a few more minutes."

The few more minutes grew to ten and Jamie was getting more and more anxious.

Then suddenly the door opened and the curator was standing there, smiling.

"Hello there. What brings you back so soon?"

"I have something for you, sir." Jamie pointed to the box.

The curator looked puzzled and walked over to the box as Jamie pulled open the lid.

"Where in the name of God did you get these?"

"A man I know has an old Hurricane and he gave these to me when I told him about yours."

"*Who* is this benefactor?" asked the curator with obvious delight.

"He doesn't want anyone to know. That's why he gave them to me."

Now the curator looked concerned.

"I really have to have some idea how you came by them before I can accept them, young man."

"You can phone my gran. She knows all about it. I didn't steal them, honest."

The curator smiled. "I'm sure you didn't, but I have to check. Do you have your grandmother's phone number?"

Jamie fished the sheet of notepaper his grandmother had given him from his pocket. "There's her address as well there, sir."

The curator gave the paper to the receptionist. "Could you get this for me, please?"

Jamie felt sure his grandmother must have been sitting by the phone, for the receptionist handed the receiver to the curator almost immediately.

After a few minutes, he put down the phone and smiled

at Jamie. "Well that's settled. Now let's have a good look at our windfall." The man lifted the dials out one by one, examining each one carefully before laying it aside.

He put the last one down slowly and turned back to Jamie who was watching anxiously.

"Well. I don't know what to say. Jamie, isn't it?"

Jamie's spirits fell with a bang. "Yes sir — aren't they any good, sir?"

"Oh yes, indeed. Every one looks in perfect condition. This is some prize you have brought us. Mrs. Jones, would you ask Mr. Burdett to come down. I want him to see what we have here."

After a few minutes, a large jovial man came through the door, an enquiring look on his face.

The curator pointed to the dials. "Take a look at these, sir. This young man brought them in."

The large man bent down and took a long look. Then he turned to Jamie. "Where did you get these, young man?" he said sternly.

"Oh, it's all right, sir. I have already checked with the boy's grandmother. They *are* his to give away."

Mr. Burdett visibly relaxed and beamed at Jamie. "Well young man, I don't know how we are going to thank you. We have been hunting for a set of these for years."

"Yes sir, I know. This man told me when I came before."

The curator broke in. "He came in a couple of weeks ago to look at the Hurricane and find out about McKnight.

Seems his grandfather wrote about him."

"Well, well, well. What are we going to do to reward you for this?"

"All I would like sir, is to see the Hurricane fly when it is finished."

"Well, that, I think we can arrange easily enough, don't you, Felix?"

"I'm sure we can," the curator replied.

"Very well, then. I'll leave that in your hands." Mr. Burdett then turned back to Jamie and put out his hand. "I can't thank you enough for this young man and I shall look forward to us meeting again."

As he left, the curator spoke again. "I will arrange for an invitation to be sent when we are ready to go, and just in case your reluctant friend changes his mind, I'll make it for two."

"Mrs. Jones," the curator turned to the receptionist, "please make a note that Jamie here has free access to the museum any time."

"Gee, thank you, sir, thanks a lot."

"That's a small reward for what you have done, Jamie."

It was at that moment Jamie looked back at the clock. "Oh gosh, I have to go. I have to be at the bus depot in half an hour."

"Don't you worry about that, Jamie. Mrs. Jones, call Eddie round and get him to run this young man to the bus depot and I'll get this precious load in to the mechanics. They are going to flip when they see these, Jamie, you can be sure. Ah, here's Eddie." The curator wrung Jamie's hand warmly. "Goodbye for now, lad, and don't forget, you can come any time to see how we are getting along."

"Thank you, sir, thank you very much."

"Oh, it's all my pleasure, I can assure you."

10

"Play Ball"

That night when Jamie picked up the notebook, he noticed that there was not much left to read. He felt sad in one way but not in another, for it seemed somehow fitting that the story was drawing to its close. He turned to his marked page and settled down on his bed.

―⁓―

It was in April of 1943 that I made my last trip back to my old street. I was due to leave for naval training the next day and had come to say goodbye to my aunt and uncle and my cousin.

It was all still there: the old square where I had smashed my first watch, playing cricket, where once we had flown a kite so high, it had taken an hour to get it down, and the spot in the middle where we had excitedly put the first match to so many giant bonfires.

And there was the shelter, where Danny and I had had our first brief brush with sex, where we had spent so many nights, telling yarns and bragging whilst the bombs rained down — but already they seemed no more than silent echoes of another life.

I turned and looked at Puddy's front gate, from where he would no more hurl sarcastic comments. Just a little way down was Sammy Napthali's house, its sparkling lace curtains hiding the strips of sticky paper, crisscrossing the windows to prevent the glass flying. But I knew that Sammy would not again come bursting out of that door, fingers trying constantly to comb his unruly hair.

Outside my Aunt Kate's was the lamppost to which my grandfather had tied up his goat, the same lamppost where once, Puddy, having just seen "Joan of Arc," tied up Sammy and set a fire around him. I had the same feeling you get when shouting in a large empty building, where, although a hundred voices appear to shout back, in reality no one is there.

———

Jamie put the notebook down and sat staring at his bedroom wall for a long time, then he suddenly got up and ran downstairs. Dragging on his coat he ran outside.

Trudging through the driving rain, he called in at the local florist. Embarrassedly tucking the flowers under his coat he headed for the cemetery. There he took the wilting bunch from the vase on his grandfather's grave and pushed his bunch quickly into it.

Then he stood up and just looked at the grave for several minutes. Suddenly he slapped his hand gently on the head-stone and said quietly, "So, what do you think, Grandpa?" Then nodding his head, as if the headstone had given him an answer, Jamie turned away.

"Hey Jamie, where you been?" Skippy yelled as Jamie approached the baseball diamond.

"Nowhere special."

Tozer grinned knowingly at Freddie. "He's got a girl. You got a girl, haven't you."

"No, I haven't got a girl."

"So what you been doing?"

"You'll find out next week in Mr. Stokes' Social Studies class. Now, you wanna play ball or what?"

ABOUT THE AUTHOR

Charles Reid was born and raised in London's East End and grew up during the Second World War. He began writing seriously some five years ago but his original dream of writing had its roots in his childhood when he had ambitions of becoming a reporter. In those days, however, working class parents did not believe careers were possible for their children and any kind of job was considered a priority. Oddly enough, it was at the time of his emigration to Canada in 1975 that the almost forgotten ambition re-surfaced. It was brought back by his discovery that the young Calgary ace who had been one of his childhood heroes was virtually unknown in his home town, even though a boulevard was named after him. Determined to bring the McKnight name to the notice of Calgarians, he started writing about the Canadian ace. Research very quickly uncovered the fact that there were many, many forgotten heroes in his new country and he set about bringing their stories to the public. Since then, he has published many articles on numerous Canadian heroes in both newspapers and military magazines. He has also published several poems with a military theme. *Hurricanes over London* is his first book but a second is already in the works. Charles Reid now makes his home in Nanaimo, British Columbia.